DOCTOR ⒹⓌ WHO
2 new adventures

—Matt Smith

D0910729

Also available:

Death Riders by Justin Richards

Heart of Stone by Trevor Baxendale

The Good the Bad and the Alien
by Colin Brake

System Wipe by Oli Smith

Sightseeing in Space
by Steve Lyons and David Bailey

Coming soon:

Monstrous Missions

by Jonathan Green and Gary Russell

Step Back in Time

by Jacqueline Rayner and Richard Dungworth

Want to get closer to the Doctor
and learn more about the very best
Doctor Who books out there?

Go to
www.doctorwhochildrensbooks.co.uk
for news, reviews, competitions
and more!

BBC Children's Books
Published by the Penguin Group
Penguin Books Ltd, 80 Strand, London, WC2R 0RL, England
Penguin Group (USA) Inc., 375 Hudson Street, New York 10014, USA
Penguin Books (Australia) Ltd, 250 Camberwell Road, Camberwell,
Victoria 3124, Australia (A division of Pearson Australia Group PTY Ltd)
Penguin Group (NZ), 67 Apollo Drive, Rosedale, North Shore
0632, New Zealand (A division of Pearson New Zealand Ltd)
Canada, India, South Africa
Published by BBC Children's Books, 2011
Text and design © Children's Character Books
The Underwater War written by Richard Dinnick
Rain of Terror written by Mike Tucker
Cover illustrations by Kev Walker and Paul Campbell
001 – 10 9 8 7 6 5 4 3 2 1
BBC logo © BBC 1996. Doctor Who logo © BBC 2009. TARDIS image © BBC 1963.
Licensed by BBC Worldwide Limited
BBC, DOCTOR WHO (word marks, logos and devices), TARDIS, DALEKS, CYBERMAN
and K-9 (word marks and devices) are trade marks of the British Broadcasting Corporation
and are used under licence.
ISBN – 978-14059-0-767-5

Mixed Sources
Product group from well-managed
forests and other controlled sources
www.fsc.org Cert no. SA-COC-1592
© 1996 Forest Stewardship Council
FSC

Printed in Great Britain by Clays Ltd, St Ives plc

DOCTOR ⓄⓌ WHO
2 new adventures

ALIEN ADVENTURES

MIKE TUCKER   RICHARD DINNICK

CONTENTS

THE UNDERWATER WAR...11

1. A SUBMARINE IN SPACE.................................13

2. THE SHOAL.................................29

3. THE UNEXPECTED VISITOR.................................43

4. MOON POOL.................................52

5. THE CELL IN THE CAVES.................................66

6. THE LOCKED DOOR.................................77

7. COLOURFUL LANGUAGE!.................................92

8. THE WATER VOLCANO.................................103

9. ADMIRAL ICKTHEUS.............................114

10. THE STAGNANT POOL.............................122

11. THE LOW SWIMMERS TAKE OVER.............131

12. THE SECRET OF THE SHOAL.................140

13. THE VERNE ESCAPES.........................150

14. MAKRON'S STORY.............................159

15. THE WRECK...................................163

16. THE DOCTOR TO THE RESCUE!.............173

17. THE FINAL MISSION.........................185

18 ARRIVALS AND DEPARTURES................197

RAIN OF TERROR 205

1. DEATH FROM THE SKY 207

2. THE COLONY 224

3. SURVIVOR 242

4. THE DOCTOR TAKES CHARGE 253

5. RUNNING OUT OF TIME 273

6. ESCAPE! 291

7. MEMORIES OF THE PAST 309

8. TRAITOR ON-BOARD 322

9. AMY IN DANGER 338

10. THE MACHINE 354

11. END OF THE LINE 370

12. FINAL SOLUTIONS 383

FOR FINLAY AND EMILY

DOCTOR WHO

THE UNDERWATER WAR

RICHARD DINNICK

CHAPTER 1
A SUBMARINE
IN SPACE

Along way from Earth there was a planet called Hydron. It was totally purple and hung in space like a big grape. The whole of this alien world was covered in water. Thin wisps of cloud moved slowly across the sky and the sea below sparkled as light from its nearby star reflected off the tips of the waves.

Around Hydron flew a very large spaceship. It was black with three long wings that stood out to either side and one at the top. It was called *The Cosmic Rover* and its name was painted on the front of the ship in big, silver letters. The lower part of the ship bulged out like a pear. This was where everything the ship needed for its mission was stored, including something you don't often find on a spacecraft.

On-board *The Cosmic Rover*, everyone was busy. The ship had arrived a few hours ago and most members of the crew were getting ready to go down to Hydron. So no one noticed the strange sound when it started to come from the storage room.

Two members of the crew walked past the storage room door just as the noise became louder, but they didn't notice it either. If they had heard it, they would have said it sounded like a strong wind, rising and falling – or perhaps a giant snoring.

It was the TARDIS arriving. The strange blue box belonged to the Doctor and as it finished appearing in the small storeroom, the door opened and a woman looked out. She had fiery, orange hair and was wearing a red jumper.

'This looks a bit small to be the Tower of London,' she said.

'Some things don't always look like they should, Amy,' said a voice from inside the TARDIS. The voice belonged to a man who now joined Amy outside. He was dressed in a tweed jacket and wore a bow tie. He looked at the crates and boxes in the cupboard. 'Ah,' he said.

Amy looked at him and bit her lip. 'No, Doctor, they don't. Do they?'

'Ah,' repeated the Doctor. 'No. No. You're right. This isn't the Tower of London.' He started jumping up and down. 'We aren't even on a planet.' He bent down and touched the floor. 'This is a spaceship. A big one. I wonder if this door is locked?'

While the Doctor went to look at the metal door a second man appeared in the doorway of the TARDIS. He had spiky hair and was wearing a green T-shirt with a black puffer jacket over the top. 'Oh,' he said. 'Not the Tower of London, then.'

'No, Rory,' the Doctor said with a frown. 'We

know that. You must keep up if you don't want to be left behind.'

Rory looked a bit hurt but knew that the Doctor didn't mean it. He knew the Doctor would never leave him behind. He went to look at the door as well. The Doctor was already shaking his head.

'Locked,' he said.

'Sonic!' said Amy, folding her arms.

The Doctor smiled. He put his hand into his jacket and pulled out the sonic screwdriver. This was the most useful tool in the universe. Among lots of other things, it could boil water and tell you if someone's heart was beating. But it was best at opening locked doors.

The sonic screwdriver looked like a thin torch with a green light at the end. The Doctor pointed it at the door and pressed the "on" button. The tool buzzed and the door clicked open.

'Come on, then! I think we should take a look around,' the Doctor said, and marched out into the corridor beyond.

At the front of the ship was the bridge, where all *The Cosmic Rover*'s systems — computers, engines and navigation — could be found. It was a square room with the two viewscreens taking up most of one side. Against the other walls were computer terminals and the ship's controls. All of the people wore overalls. Each section of the crew had a different coloured overall: blue for the main crew, black for security and white for medical and scientific.

The ship's captain, Jane Clancy, sat in the command chair. She wore navy blue overalls with four gold stripes on her sleeves that told everyone her rank. Her soft, brown eyes stared out from her chocolate coloured skin, looking around at the other people on the bridge. She ran a hand through her curly black hair. Then she put her captain's baseball cap on her head in an attempt to keep her hair tidy.

Around her, several of her crew were seated at computer screens, making final changes to the controls. They had to fly the ship into an exact position above the watery planet. Everyone was concentrating on their work really hard, so they didn't notice the three new people enter the room.

'Hello,' said the Doctor with a lopsided grin. Everyone looked up.

'Who are you?' the captain demanded, rising from her chair. 'What are you doing on my ship?'

A man with very pale skin and wearing a black uniform stood up. He took a gun from a holster on his belt. 'Stay where you are!' he said.

'It's all right,' the Doctor continued. 'I'm the Doctor. This is Amy and Rory.'

Clancy looked at them. 'You can't be pirates,' she said.

'No. Not pirates,' Amy agreed.

'How did you get onboard?' asked the man in black.

The Doctor walked up to him and read the name that was printed on his uniform.

'Mister Fleming? Excellent. Good question,

Mister Fleming. You are head of security, I take it?'

'Correct,' said Fleming.

'Good,' said the Doctor. 'Always alert, looking for danger. But we're not dangerous. So you can put the gun away, please.'

The captain nodded and Fleming lowered his weapon.

The Doctor smiled at him and said, 'Thank you.'

'You still need to answer my question: how did you get aboard?'

'Ah. Long range matter transmitter. We beamed in straight from Head Office,' the Doctor said. 'All very secret, of course. You might not know about it...' He smiled. 'Yes. So we're from Head Office. I'm in charge of Health and Safety. Anyway, we're here to help.'

Amy looked confused. What was the Doctor talking about? She glanced at Rory who shrugged.

The Doctor had taken out a small wallet and opened it to show the crew what was inside. It looked like blank paper behind a plastic covering but Amy knew this was the psychic paper.

The psychic paper showed people whatever the Doctor wanted them to see. If he had to pretend he had a ticket for travelling on a train or bus, he could use the psychic paper. If he wanted to get into a top secret army base, he could use the psychic paper. Like the sonic screwdriver, it was a very useful piece of kit.

'What are you a doctor of, exactly?' asked the captain.

'And who are you?' asked the Doctor, spinning round. He stared at the woman.

'I am Captain Jane Clancy.'

'Wonderful. Captain Jane! I like it,' the Doctor smiled. There was a small pause. 'Oh, I'm a doctor of almost everything. What's your mission here?'

'Don't you know?' asked Fleming.

'They didn't tell us about that,' said the Doctor. 'No time. They just sent us to keep an eye on things!'

'Really?' asked Fleming, looking a little nervous.

'We were just going to run through our last minute checks for the drop,' Clancy replied.

'Drop?' asked Amy.

'The sub,' replied Fleming. 'You must know about that!'

'Of course we do,' the Doctor bluffed.

'Dropping a sub. . . submarine. Right?' asked Rory.

'That is what we do for a water planet like Hydron,' said Clancy.

'Thank you,' said the Doctor. He turned and pointed Amy and Rory to spare seats. They sat and listened as the captain told them about the mission.

'As you know, the planet Hydron is a world almost completely covered in water,' Captain Jane explained. 'There are only a few rocky islands in the sea and even those have fresh water lakes taking up most of the room on them. So, we can't build a normal base on the planet. Instead we have to use a submarine, which we've brought from Earth.'

'Ah! That's why the hold is so big!' the Doctor exclaimed.

'The submarine is an Under Sea Exploration Ship and its name is *The Ocean Explorer*,' said Clancy. 'The Company has sent us to examine the fresh water lakes. According to my mission briefing, some interesting minerals have been detected there that we can use.'

'So you haven't been here before?' asked Amy.

'No,' Fleming said quickly.

'The Company told me that the minerals were detected by a satellite,' Captain Jane smiled. 'Anyway, the submarine will be dropped into the sea from space. The sub is protected against the heat of the planet's atmosphere. We will then use parachutes to slow us down before we hit the water. We don't expect there will be any difficulties.'

'Not before we get there,' muttered Fleming under his breath. The Doctor glanced at him but said nothing.

Clancy also looked at her security officer. Then

she looked at Amy. 'Are you a marine expert?'

The Doctor jumped up again. 'She certainly is. With a name like "Pond" she must know something about water...'

'It's not "Pond",' said Rory. 'It's "Williams".' No one took any notice.

'I know quite a lot about the sea myself,' the Doctor said. 'Pescatons, Sea Devils, Skarasen, Myrka.' He lowered his voice. 'Even went to Atlantis once. Or was it twice? Anyway. Yes. You could say I'm an expert.'

'Good,' the captain smiled. 'We'll be leaving within the hour.'

The meeting came to an end. Captain Clancy stood up.

As her crew began to leave, another woman went up to Fleming. She wore white overalls and had her blonde hair pulled back into a bun. She whispered something to the head of security and then waved her arms about as if she was angry or perhaps scared.

'Don't worry, Doctor Morton,' Fleming said quietly but firmly. 'Nothing will go wrong.'

The Doctor watched the hushed conversation and then followed Amy and Rory from the room. He caught up with his companions and together they followed the small team of people down a corridor to a lift. The lift took them down several decks until it opened onto the huge cargo hold.

Suspended from the ceiling, and held by two giant, metal clamps, was the submarine. It was about the length of a football stadium and as tall as a house, with a tower that stood up above that by another five metres or so. The tower had a doorway in its side with a thick metal door that led to a ramp. A handful of crew were carrying aboard the last few boxes of supplies for the mission. On top of the tower an engineer was adjusting the aerial that stood next to a periscope, sticking out from the roof.

Although it looked like most submarines Amy had ever seen, *The Ocean Explorer* had large fins sticking out from either side at the back and front. More crewmen dressed in blue stood on these fins or were suspended from scaffolding so they could carry out their last minute checks.

'Wow,' said Amy.

'That's a big submarine,' added Rory.

'It is, isn't it?' the Doctor said with a smile. 'Let's go onboard!'

An hour later, the Doctor, Amy and Rory were sitting in a large room at the front of the submarine. It was behind the sub's control room and Rory could see Captain Clancy and Fleming through the large hatchway that connected the two cabins. Like the others, Rory was strapped into one of the white leather chairs that lined the sides of the room.

The three had been given yellow overalls to wear by the captain, although the Doctor had decided against it. He continued to wear his tweed jacket and bow tie. 'Bow ties,' he had explained to the captain, 'are cool.'

As he sat there, Rory counted the forty seats that lined the walls. Apart from the people who had to be in the control room or the engine room, every other member of *The Ocean Explorer*'s crew was there. Most were wearing blue uniforms, but there were quite a lot of people in black overalls, too. Rory wondered why a scientific mission needed so many security guards.

He shrugged at his own thoughts and then saw the woman who had been making a fuss earlier, Doctor Morton. She walked towards the chair next to Rory's and sat down.

'Hello,' he said, looking sideways at the blonde.

She looked at him and smiled but said nothing.

'Right...' He smiled back. 'I'm Rory,' he continued. 'Are you a medical doctor?'

Finally she spoke. 'I am,' she said. 'Are you?'

'Oh. No. I'm a nurse. Well, I was,' he shrugged. 'But then I've also been a Roman soldier and a security guard.'

'A Roman soldier?' she asked.

'It's a long story,' Rory said. There was a pause.

'Well,' said Doctor Morton. 'If I need an assistant, I'll let you know.'

She turned round and started speaking with the woman sitting next to her.

'That went well,' said Rory quietly. He sighed. Before he could work out why Doctor Morton didn't seem to like him, an alarm began to sound. The crew all tensed.

'DOWN DROP IN TWO MINUTES,' said a computer voice.

Heavy thuds could be heard on the hull of the sub as the giant claws moved the submarine into position and Rory felt the ship bump a bit as it was jolted down. A low droning sound filled the room and then he heard something like a rushing wind.

'They're opening the spacecraft's outer doors,' the Doctor explained.

Rory nodded. The alarm sounded again.

'DOWN DROP IN ONE MINUTE,' said the

computer.

Amy looked at the Doctor and Rory. She had a big grin on her face. She blew out her cheeks and then made an "eek" sound.

'It's not a fairground ride, Pond,' said the Doctor.

'Isn't it?' she asked cheekily.

'More like a parachute jump!' the Doctor said. The alarm went off for a third time and this time it didn't stop.

'DOWN DROP IN 30 SECONDS,' said a computer voice. 'RETRACTING FINS.'

There was a mechanical whine as the submarine's fins were pulled inside the boat's main body. Everyone took this as a sign to grip the arms of their chairs as they prepared themselves for the drop. Rory gulped. He'd never done a parachute jump.

Then the computer started the final countdown, talking over the top of the noisy alarm: '5... 4... 3... 2... 1... DOWN DROP!'

The Doctor smiled. 'Geronimo!'

CHAPTER 2
THE SHOAL

The claws released the submarine and it fell away from *The Cosmic Rover* as if someone had dropped a brick off a cliff. Rory's stomach lurched. He felt like he was travelling to the basement in the fastest lift ever built from the top floor of the tallest skyscraper.

For a few seconds the submarine was still in space and Rory felt that he was going to float out of his seat, but the seatbelt kept him in place. Then the submarine was rattling and shaking. He could feel the air becoming warmer. Both were the result of entering the planet's atmosphere. The noise from outside was so loud Rory could hardly hear anything else.

Except Amy. She was holding her arms up, shouting and smiling as if she was on a rollercoaster. The Doctor looked calm – almost a little bored. He'd obviously done this type of thing loads of times. Rory just swallowed and kept his eyes shut tight.

Outside, the sub was starting to glow light orange as it fell. Then, as the sky around the ship turned from black to purple, the heat began to decrease. The submarine was travelling at well over one hundred miles per hour, zipping through the clouds of the planet Hydron.

Rory could feel the heat dying away now. Then he realised he had been holding his breath and he slowly let the air out of his mouth. 'Phew!' he said and opened his eyes.

'PARACHUTES IN 5... 4... 3...

'Hold on!' the Doctor called over the noise of the wind.

The submarine suddenly jerked and if it hadn't been for the seatbelts, Rory was sure he would have hit the ceiling of the room.

'DEPLOYING FINS,' the computer voice announced.

The Doctor smiled. 'It's OK, Rory. The fins will act like breaks. They'll slow us down ready for splashdown.' He gave Rory a thumbs up.

In the calm waters of the purple sea far below, a creature rose to the surface. He looked like a fish but he was larger than a man, with stripes of brown and cream on his body. His name was Makron and he was a member of the Shoal, the beings who lived on Hydron.

Makron turned his face to the sun and closed his eyes. The pattern of fins on his cheeks fluttered as they felt its warmth. It was peaceful and relaxing. Then, suddenly, there was a whistling sound from above.

The Shoaly opened his eyes and saw the dark shape of the submarine falling towards him. The parachutes above the sub looked like huge grey jellyfish in the sky. Makron's eyes widened in horror and he dived back beneath the waves. He was terrified but he knew he had to tell his people about this.

Makron swam down through the purple water, passing many different types of animal on his way down. Finally he reached the kelp fields that stretched away in every direction. The tall, red and brown seaweed waved in the ocean currents. Makron could see several other Shoaly working or travelling through the farmland.

He swam faster as soon as he found the underwater road. Because the Shoal did not move on the seabed, the roads on Hydron were not hard and smooth. Instead they were a collection of coloured shells and stones that acted as guides, leading the Shoal to different destinations. This one led to the Shoal's capital city – Reef.

Reef was a natural mountain of coral that had been carved and built on by the Shoal. It was protected by a steep, hard rock face that was guarded day and night. Now Makron approached the undersea cliff. The water had worn away at a crack in the stone and formed a natural tunnel. This was the main entrance to Reef and two other Shoaly were floating either side of it.

These were the low swimmers; the fish that had evolved deep in the oceans of Hydron and they looked very different from Makron. The low swimmers were coloured dark brown with grey stripes. They had very big mouths and strange, golden eyes that looked like they were about to pop out of their heads.

The most unusual thing about them was their "lure". This was a small, glowing ball that hung from a piece of skin between their eyes. It could be used to hypnotise and, because its glow was caused by the low swimmer's natural electricity, it could also be used to stun or even kill other Shoaly.

Makron came to a stop and let the guards wave their lures over him, checking for anything odd or out of place. Makron's cheeks pulsed with an orange colour, telling the guards that he was in a hurry. Like most Shoaly, the low swimmers did not wear many clothes, but they did have belts around their waists. The belts had two pieces of equipment and a forked weapon hanging on them. Because Makron was simply entering the city, there was no need for them to use the weapons or scanners. A small flash of dull white on the nearest guard's face told Makron that he could pass.

Makron moved down the tunnel, passing other members of the Shoal: high swimmers like himself, and medium swimmers who were much more colourful. His father called them "loud" and disapproved of them. Makron wasn't so sure about that, but it was his father he needed to see now.

The Shoal was looked after by an Assembly made up of high swimmers. His father was one of the Shoaly in charge of a region, called a

Governor. Makron had to tell him what he had seen falling from the sky and he knew where his father would be.

The city of Reef was beautiful. It had no pollution and no square buildings. All its structures were natural or had been built to look natural. The city was formed out of layers. The lower you went, the darker it became. That was where some of the low swimmers lived. Most of them lived outside Reef, deeper in the ocean in towns called Pools.

The highest point of Reef was a cone of bright orange coral decorated with different coloured seaweeds, each one representing one of the many regions of Hydron. This was where the regional governors gathered to meet and talk about how to run the planet. All the entrances to the Assembly building were guarded by the dangerous-looking low swimmers.

As Makron neared them, one of the low swimmers flashed red at him. This was a warning.

Its face changed again to grey with a bit of yellow. This told anyone watching that this was a security check and that Makron should be careful. He slowed down and came to a stop in front of the low swimmers. He told them that he was in a hurry (orange) and that his father (yellow) was a member of the Assembly (black and purple).

One of the low swimmers took a machine from his belt. It was triangular and shimmered like a butterfly's wing, all the colours of the rainbow. The guard scanned Makron with the device and it flashed white, confirming that his father did work there. The low swimmer nodded at Makron and the young Shoaly swam past quickly.

There were no doors in the Assembly building but most of the spaces between the arms of the coral had flat seaweed curtains so no one could see what was going on inside the rooms. Makron arrived at his father's office and burst through the curtain. His father was a large Shoaly with very clear stripes of light brown and dark cream.

'*What are you doing?*' his father, Darkin, asked, flashing red and black with anger.

Makron twinkled with blue, green and pink. '*I'm sorry, Dad.*'

'*Why have you rushed in here? What is so important?*' Red – purple – black.

Makron paused. He wasn't sure his dad would believe him. He frowned. '*They're back,*' he said. Red: danger. Brown: return. Violet: alien!

The submarine hit the water and sank into the purple waves for a second before bobbing up again, moving slowly from side to side. The large, grey parachutes that had slowed down the submarine floated down. Two of them landed in the sea while the third fell over the tower. It almost looked like the submarine had pulled a blanket over itself, ready for bed.

In the control room, Captain Clancy stared out of the viewscreen and nodded. Good. They had made it. She turned to one of her crew and ordered him to bring the parachutes back in. He pressed a few buttons on his computer and the winch that was connected to the parachutes started winding in the canopies. As they were pulled back inside the sub, a special machine squeezed the water out of the material.

'Parachutes in,' said the sailor.

Captain Clancy nodded. 'Very good,' she said. 'Prepare to dive!' She turned round and found herself face to face with the Doctor.

'Are we in a hurry, Captain Jane?' he asked, looking out of the viewscreen. 'I mean, there's a lovely purple sea out there. Couldn't we have a look at that first?'

'This isn't a tourist trip, Doctor,' she replied. 'We have a mission to complete! I need to get this submarine to one of the freshwater lakes as quickly as I can. The report I was given before the mission also said there were dangerous sea creatures here!'

'Did you say that the report was based on what

a satellite found here?' the Doctor smiled.

'That's right,' she said. 'It performed a scan of the planet and detected both useful mineral deposits and the hostile life forms.'

'The satellite was in space?' the Doctor came closer, peering at Captain Clancy.

Captain Clancy looked uncomfortable. 'Of course,' she said.

'So where is the satellite now?'

'I suppose the Company must have collected it and taken it back to Earth,' Clancy smiled weakly. 'I'm just employed to do my job, Doctor, not to know all the ins and outs of how the Company works.'

'Yes. I can see that,' the Doctor said. 'It's just interesting, isn't it?'

'What is?'

'That a machine in space can tell whether a creature under the sea is dangerous and hostile.'

Before Clancy could reply, a crewmember came up and interrupted her.

'All systems are ready, Captain,' the sailor said.

'Excuse me, Doctor,' Clancy said as she walked away from him to talk to her crew. A man and a woman sat at the front of the control room, under the screen. They were driving the submarine. Four others stood at the two side walls, pressing buttons to turn on the sub's engines.

'Not hanging around, then?' asked Amy. She walked up and stood beside the Doctor and looked out at the strange sea.

'No,' the Doctor said. 'It looks like Captain Jane is in a hurry for some reason.'

'Ahead one third!' Clancy called. The crew who were standing up started turning controls.

'Five degree down bubble!' called the captain.

'What on earth does that mean?' asked Rory.

Slowly, the floor of *The Ocean Explorer* began to tilt. Amy and Rory held onto each other so that they didn't fall over.

'It means we're going under water,' the Doctor said. He looked at Amy. 'I think we should investigate. There's something not right here. People are keeping secrets – and I think we should start with Mister Fleming and Doctor Morton.'

The corridors in the submarine were painted white and had pipes running down them. They carried fresh water and air to all the cabins so that the crew could breathe, drink and wash. The Doctor walked beside Rory and Amy pointing to the different rooms as they passed.

'At the front of the submarine is the control room,' he said. 'That sits over the sonar system.'

'Sonar is like underwater radar, right?' asked Rory.

'That's right,' replied the Doctor. 'They use it to see things like whales and other submarines and stuff.' The Doctor ducked under a particularly fat pipe. 'So, above the control room you have the "sail"; the tower that sticks up from the rest of the sub. That's where the periscope and radio antenna are. Where we are now is the mess.'

'Mess?' asked Amy. 'It looks tidy to me.'

'The mess is what the military or the navy call the kitchen and dining room.'

The Doctor sat down at one of the silver tables. Rory and Amy joined him.

'I don't know what's going on here,' whispered the Doctor. 'But I think we need to find out as much as we can from different people.'

The Doctor explained that he was going to speak to Mister Fleming, the head of security. 'I think you should stick with Captain Jane, Amy,' he said.

'What about me?' asked Rory, looking a little hurt.

'Don't worry. You are going to see Doctor Morton.'

'Oh,' said Rory, remembering that she didn't seem to like him. 'Great.'

CHAPTER 3
THE UNEXPECTED VISITOR

The security centre was towards the back of the submarine. It was a large room that had a lot of screens showing pictures from cameras in different parts of *The Ocean Explorer*. There was a desk with computer controls and a locked storage cupboard of weapons. In one of the side walls was a doorway that led to a group of four small cells. This was the "brig".

The Doctor entered the room and smiled at Fleming who was sitting at the desk. The thin man looked up and frowned.

'Can I help you, Doctor?' he asked. It didn't sound like he meant it.

'I think you can!' the Doctor grinned. 'You see, I heard what you said to Doctor Morton during the meeting earlier.'

The Doctor walked round the desk and looked at the screens. Fleming stood up.

'What do you mean?'

'Are you expecting trouble, Mister Fleming?' asked the Doctor. He didn't look at Fleming. Instead he stared at a screen that showed Rory walking down a corridor.

'I am Head of Security,' said Fleming. 'It's my job to look for trouble.'

'Ah, yes. Well I can understand that.' The Doctor turned to look at him. He narrowed his eyes. 'But you're not looking for it. You know it's going to happen, don't you?'

Fleming opened his mouth to speak but before he could say a word, a warning sounded.

BLEEP. BLEEP. BLEEP.

'See?' said the Doctor.

'It's the rear hatch!' Fleming snatched his gun

from the desk and ran from the room. He shouted into a radio as he ran, 'Jason! Nick! Get to the rear hatch! Something's opening it!'

The Doctor nodded to himself and then ran after Fleming.

Suddenly, there was a "boom" from far away and the submarine lurched to one side. The Doctor was thrown against the wall and fell to the floor on his knees. He looked up. 'Oh, dear!' he said.

Straight away a loud alarm went off.

'HULL BREACH! HULL BREACH!' announced the computer voice.

The Doctor stood up and ran down the corridor towards the back of the submarine.

'This is the captain!' Clancy's voice came over the submarine's public address system. 'Engineers to the rear hatch. Crew, prepare to close flood doors!'

The submarine lurched again but the Doctor managed to stay on his feet. He jumped through a hatch and landed in water. It was about as deep as a paddling pool. Ahead of him Fleming was talking to Rory outside the medical bay.

'What's happening?' called the Doctor.

'Doctor Morton has been attacked!' said Rory, pointing to a bunk in the medical bay where she was lying.

'Is she okay?' asked the Doctor.

Rory nodded. 'I scared off the thing that was attacking her.'

'You saw it?' The Doctor grabbed Rory by the shoulders. 'What did it look like?'

'He *says* he saw it,' said Fleming. 'We only have his word for that.'

'Are you suggesting that Rory attacked Doctor Morton?' asked the Doctor. 'Don't be ridiculous. This is my friend. He wouldn't lie.' He looked at Fleming.

'Thank you,' said Rory.

'So what did it look like, Rory?' the Doctor asked as he bent down and pulled out the sonic screwdriver. It made a buzzing sound as he waved it over the body of Doctor Morton. 'She'll live,' he said.

'It was big,' Rory said. 'Bigger than me. It looked sort of like a fish but it had great big, bulging eyes. It was walking like a sea lion – on four kind of flippers, but the front ones looked like they had fingers.'

'Interesting!' the Doctor whispered. 'Come on!'

'Where are you going?' shouted Fleming.

The Doctor ran out of the door and sped up the corridor, splashing through the water. 'It might still be onboard!' he shouted back.

Rory and Fleming looked at one another. Rory shook his head. 'I'll stay here and look after the patient. You go!'

Fleming hesitated for a moment and then ran after the Doctor, catching him up just as he reached a closed door. A crewman stood beside it.

'When did you shut this?' demanded the Doctor.

'Just now,' replied the sailor, frowning.

'Well, open it again!'

'No!' Fleming looked at the Doctor. 'If we open that door, the submarine will be flooded. We'll sink.'

'We need to speak to that creature!' The Doctor looked at the sailor and then at Fleming. Neither of them moved.

'REAR HATCH SECURE. SUBMARINE SAFE,' the computer announced.

'Drain the sea water!' said Captain Clancy over the loud speaker.

The Doctor shook his head and turned away from the door.

In the control room Amy was watching the captain. She was impressed. Clancy had reacted well to the emergency. She had quickly given orders and made sure that the submarine was safe. Amy found that she liked the woman.

Then the Doctor marched in. His eyes flashed with anger. 'You know what is going on here and I demand to be told!' he said. 'Sea creatures do not open hatches and attack the crew for no reason.'

Captain Clancy looked at the Doctor as if he were mad. 'I don't know what you're talking about Doctor,' she said. 'Really.'

'Captain, I think you and your entire crew are in danger and someone onboard knows why.' The Doctor leant forward and stared into her brown eyes. 'You can tell me,' he said gently.

Just then, Fleming entered the room. He looked at the Doctor and then the captain. 'What's going on?' he asked.

'That is exactly what I want to know, Mister Fleming,' the Doctor said. 'Why were we attacked just now?'

'Like the report says, this planet has hostile life forms,' Fleming said.

'Humans!' exclaimed the Doctor.

'I'm one, too,' Amy said, putting her hands on her hips. 'What have you done with my husband?'

'He's in the medical bay. He's looking after

Doctor Morton. She's been attacked by a fish creature.'

'Wow. Really?'

'Yes, really,' the Doctor said, looking over at Captain Clancy. His eyes narrowed and then he smiled. 'Captain Jane!' she looked up at him. 'I want to have a look outside.'

'What?' said Amy and Clancy, together. The two women exchanged looks.

The Doctor explained that because he was a very important person from Head Office, he could ask the captain of *The Ocean Explorer* to do whatever he wanted – as long as it didn't put the ship in danger. 'I want to see what's out there. Or who's out there,' he said. 'If you've got fish creatures sneaking aboard, then I'd like to find out why.'

Fleming's eyes narrowed to slits but he didn't say a word.

'Very well, Doctor,' Captain Jane said. 'If you want to have a look outside we can switch on the camera feeds from here.'

She moved over to a row of controls behind her chair.

'No,' said the Doctor. 'No, no, no. I don't want to watch TV. I'm more of a "get up and go" rather than a "sit down and stop" sort of person! I want to get out there!' he pointed at the screen and the dark, purple waters it showed.

'All right,' the captain sighed. 'Mister Fleming, show the Doctor to *The Verne*.'

The Doctor smiled. 'That's more like it!'

Amy rushed forward. 'I'm coming too.'

CHAPTER 4
MOON POOL

Fleming took the Doctor and Amy down a staircase in the corner of the control room. It was so steep, Amy thought it was more like a ladder than a flight of steps. They climbed down two decks from the control room and emerged into a large area that was brightly lit.

There were cupboards and lockers against the walls. Amy could see orange diving suits hanging in them along with bits of diving equipment. At the far end was a small yellow submersible that looked like it could fit about four people inside.

However, the most impressive part of the room was what Fleming called the "Moon Pool".

It was a circle of water that was open to the sea. Fleming explained that to stop the submarine being crushed by the water around it, the air had to be kept at a certain pressure. This meant that — as long as that pressure was maintained – the water could not get in through the pool.

Amy looked confused.

'Did you ever play with empty shampoo or bubble bath bottles in the tub?' asked the Doctor. Amy nodded. 'You can hold a plastic bottle upside down in the bath with the cap off. If you push the bottle down, the water doesn't get in. The air keeps it out.'

Amy looked at the pool. She found it hard to believe that the water didn't just rush in and flood into the submarine.

Fleming walked to where the yellow submarine was sitting on a platform on the other side of the Moon Pool. The Doctor and Amy followed him and looked at the small sub. It had a big, round window at the front and several robotic arms on its side. Amy thought it looked a little like a yellow crab. Then she saw that behind this sub there was another. She pointed this out to the Doctor.

'Yes, we have two submersibles,' explained Fleming. 'The bigger one is *The Verne* and the smaller one is *The Jules*.

'One of my favourite writers,' the Doctor said, running a hand along the smooth metal of *The Verne*'s hull. 'He wrote *20,000 Leagues Under the Sea* – all about a submarine. Wonderful stuff. Very wild imagination. And that Nemo, eh? What a villain! Did you know that "Nemo" means "no one" in Latin?'

'Nemo?' asked Amy. 'Wasn't he a Disney character?'

'Not the clownfish!' the Doctor said. 'You can't have a clownfish in a submarine, sinking the world's sailing ships. That would be silly.'

'Obviously,' Amy said.

Fleming looked at them both. 'You'll find diving suits over there. Change into them and then

I can get you loaded into *The Verne*.'

Ten minutes later, the Doctor and Amy were dressed in the orange diving suits and carrying helmets that had small lights on the side, to show up whatever the person wearing it was looking at. They climbed up the ladder on the side of the sub and into *The Verne*'s cockpit through a small airlock.

There wasn't much room in the submersible but the Doctor and Amy took up the two seats in front of the round windscreen. There were two smaller seats behind this but as no one else was coming with them, Amy put her helmet there and the Doctor did the same. Then, the Time Lord closed the hatch and screwed it shut tightly. There was a click as safety bolts locked the hatch.

'It's been a while since I drove one of these,' he said, wiggling his fingers.

Through the window, Amy watched as Fleming went to stand by a bank of controls. He pressed a button and spoke. 'Are you ready?' His voice came over the radio.

The Doctor pressed down his communication button. 'All set!' he said, grinning.

Fleming nodded and flicked some switches. There was a hiss as the hydraulic arms pushed forward the platform that *The Verne* was standing on. When the sub was completely over the Moon Pool, the platform lowered it into the sea water.

Amy saw the water level rising. It reached the glass screen and then bubbled past until the sea closed over the sub.

'Okay,' said Fleming. 'You can keep in contact by using the radio, but you're on your own now.'

'So, we're looking for fish, then?'

'Not fish, Amelia,' the Doctor said staring through the screen. 'That's like calling humans "monkeys".'

'Okay then. Fish people,' Amy said. 'Where do we find them?'

The Doctor looked at Amy and smiled. 'What is a fish's favourite party game?'

'What?' Amy frowned. 'Is this a joke?'

'Yes. What is a fish's favourite party game?'

'I don't know. Tell me.'

'Tide and seek!' The Doctor laughed and pushed the control stick down.

Amy shook her head. 'That is the worst joke I've ever heard!' she said, but she couldn't help smiling.

The Doctor's eyes twinkled and *The Verne* jerked away from the circle of the Moon Pool and dived down into the darker water below.

Rory was in the submarine's medical bay. He was wearing a surgical mask and was looking at Doctor Morton as he held her wrist, taking her pulse. She was lying on a bunk surrounded by a see-through plastic tent. Her breathing was fast, almost like a dog panting.

Rory bent down to look at Doctor Morton's face. She was sweating because of her high temperature. 'Can you hear me?' Rory said. 'I need to give you some medicine. Do you have anything for fever?'

Doctor Morton opened her eyes and licked her dry lips. 'Security pass,' she said and half lifted a hand in the direction of a desk and computer that sat on other side of the room. Rory went over and found what looked like a credit card. It had a picture of Doctor Morton and her name was printed underneath. Rory saw that her first name was Angela.

'Is this it, Angela?' he asked.

She nodded her head once. 'Use it to open the cupboards,' she said.

Rory went over to the nearest medical locker. Below the handle there was a small panel. When Rory put the pass on the panel, it opened the cupboard. Rory smiled. Very useful, he thought.

He searched each cupboard and quickly found the right medicine cabinet for the equipment he was looking for. He found a spray syringe and filled it with a capsule of a medicine that he recognised.

He came back to Doctor Morton and gently took her hand. 'I've found something to get your temperature down, Angela,' he said. 'It'll also help you sleep.' He pressed the syringe against her arm. 'It will help your body recover from the attack.'

Doctor Morton looked at him. 'Be careful,' she said.

Rory frowned. 'Don't worry,' he said. 'I'm a nurse. Remember?'

She shook her head and whispered something. Rory thought it sounded like "row". Then she fell asleep.

Just then, Captain Clancy came in.

'How is she?' Clancy asked.

'I think she'll be OK,' Rory said. 'But I'm just a nurse.'

'Doctor Morton is the only medical officer on my crew,' Clancy told him. 'You are the best person to take care of her. Some of the crew know a bit of first aid, but you have proper medical training.'

Rory looked at her. There were plenty of crew

aboard. There were sailors and a lot of security guards. 'That's a bit mad, isn't it?' Rory asked. 'I mean, only one doctor? What would happen if I wasn't here?'

'Well, there is a Robot Medic,' Captain Clancy said. She quickly explained that if there was an emergency, every submarine had a robot that could be used. It wasn't programmed to do what a doctor could do, but it could help.

'Where is it, then?' asked Rory.

Ten minutes later, the robot was standing in the medical bay. Two engineers had brought it in and hurriedly assembled its three main parts. The bottom bit looked like a tank. It was thick and heavy because that is where its motor was, and it had a track either side so it could move and four small headlights at the front that were switched off. Its middle part was as wide as Rory's chest and had lots of compartments where pills, medicines and tools were kept.

Above this were the robot's shoulders. It had

two thin arms that ended in three metal fingers. In between its arms was a small computer screen where medical information could be displayed. At the moment it was showing a green crescent moon painted on its chest. Rory guessed this was the space equivalent of the Red Cross.

The machine's neck started at the height of Rory's waist. It was as thick as a lamppost and jointed in several places. On top of this was the Robot Medic's head. It had two, large square lenses for eyes and a small round speaker for a mouth.

'Greetings,' said the robot in a male, sing-song voice. 'I am Medical Assistance Robot Vehicle for use in Emergencies. If it is easier you can call me "MARVE".'

The engineers left and Captain Clancy sat down at the small table. 'Will Doctor Morton be all right?' she asked.

'I think so,' Rory said. 'Whatever attacked her left a nasty burn on her cheek.' He pointed to Doctor Morton's face, which was red from where something had hit her. 'By the looks of it, I think something gave her an electric shock.'

'What's the tent for?'

'That? Oh, well, it looks like the wound has an infection. I checked on the computer and it told me to put that up. It's called a Biological Hazard Tent.'

'Could it spread?' asked Clancy. She looked worried.

'Honestly? I don't know,' said Rory. He was concerned, too. 'I'll be watching her very closely.'

'Thank you,' said the captain. 'I am sure you and MARVE, here, can keep things under control.'

She stood up and patted MARVE on the head and left the medical bay. Rory looked at the robot. The robot looked at Rory.

'Are you just going to sit there?' asked the robot.

'What?' Rory stared at MARVE. 'Great! A robot with attitude. That's all I need.'

Several thousand feet away from where Rory was

sitting, *The Verne* moved slowly through the dark purple depths of the sea. The Doctor was steering the submersible while peering through the window at the area of water that was illuminated by the sub's headlights.

Amy was looking at a round sonar screen. A yellow line swept round in a circle. Every time it found something larger than two feet long or wide it made a "ping" sound very loudly. The Doctor would then take the sub to have a look at whatever the machine had detected. So far they had found a rainbow-coloured jellyfish, a large crab-like animal with ten legs and a blob of floating water plants.

'Why was the sand wet?' he asked, still staring at the mass of kelp and other vegetation.

'Is this going to be another of your rubbish jokes?' Amy asked, folding her arms.

'Because the sea weed!' The Doctor looked sideways at her, a grin spreading across his face. Amy rolled her eyes but smiled, too. She had to admit that it was quite funny.

Without warning, the light in *The Verne* went off. All the power was gone. An orange emergency light came on and Amy grabbed the Doctor's arm.

'Steady, Pond,' he said. 'This might be just what we're looking for.'

Together they stared through the window, trying to see anything in the gloom of the waters outside.

Suddenly there was a flash of bright red light a few metres away from the sub. Amy jumped.

'What's that?' She sounded frightened.

Before the Doctor could answer, the first flash was joined by another and another until there was a whole army of pulsing red lights. In the glow they gave off, Amy could see that the lights belonged to a crowd of fish.

'They're making the lights flash with their skin,' Amy said quietly. 'How are they doing that?'

'Bio-luminescence,' the Doctor replied. 'It's when an animal makes light by using the chemicals in its body. Like fireflies or glow-worms.'

'Or giant fish.'

'Deep sea creatures on Earth can do it, too,' the Doctor added. Amy looked at him. He was staring at the light show like a toddler in a toy shop. 'It's beautiful,' he said.

Then, the fish charged.

CHAPTER 5
THE CELL IN THE CAVES

In the medical bay, Angela Morton's condition was getting worse. The mark on the side of her face had turned from red to bright yellow. Worse, the infection had spread though her veins making her face look like someone had drawn a pattern like a tree's root system on it.

Rory was now wearing a white suit and hood with a mask and goggles, as well as boots and gloves. They were all sealed so that he looked like he was wearing a spacesuit. This was so the disease could not infect him.

He climbed inside the plastic tent and stood beside the bed, looking with concern at the woman who lay there. Then he bent down and dabbed a small towel soaked in cold water on her face. Angela murmured the same word – row – in her sleep but she did not wake up.

Rory wondered what she was talking about. Was she referring to a rowing boat? Did she want to row away from the submarine or something? He couldn't figure out what she meant so he turned round to speak with MARVE.

'It's an alien virus,' Rory said. 'Should we take a sample? Analyse it or something?'

'It would be a start,' MARVE replied.

'If I give it to you, can you look at it? Work out what it is and stuff?'

'Affirmative.'

Rory nodded. He removed a small plastic jar from his bio-suit and unscrewed the top. Then he took a medical swab and wiped the material gently on Angela's face. He popped the swab into the jar and put the top back on.

He left the tent and took off his hood with a sigh

of relief. Then he passed the sample of the virus to MARVE. The Robo-Medic took the jar with one of his thin, metal hands and moved over to the bench on which sat various pieces of medical equipment. The robot put the virus sample into a machine that looked like a microwave and closed the door.

Just then, the hatch flew open and two crewmen entered carrying another man. They put him on a bunk and told Rory that he had collapsed in the engine room. Rory looked at his name tag. It read "Luke Garlick". He was trying to talk, but Rory calmed him down and rolled up the man's sleeve. There were several yellow streaks running up his arm from the wrist to the elbow.

Rory looked at the two men who had carried their friend. 'It's spreading,' he said.

Quickly, he contacted the captain on the radio and told her what was happening.

'You're the chief medical officer,' Clancy told Rory. 'What do we do?'

Rory thought for a second. He didn't know

how this virus was spreading. Sometimes viruses spread by people touching each other or other surfaces. The worst viruses were passed from person to person in the air – by people coughing and sneezing.

'Have any of the crew reported that they have colds?' asked Rory.

There was a silence on the radio while Captain Clancy thought about this. 'No. I don't think so.'

'Good!' Rory sighed. 'Then we can assume that this virus is spread through touch. We need to collect all the people who have touched Doctor Morton since the attack – and this man, too,' he explained. 'Then you need to scrub this sub until it shines with anti-viral cleaner. Once we've done that we should be safe.'

'Should be?'

'Yeah, well, you see there might be walls or doors or bits of engine that Luke here might have touched that other people have now touched, too.'

'Are you saying that we don't have this under

control?'

'Yes. Yes, I am,' said Rory.

'Great,' said the captain.

'There's one more thing,' Rory added.

'What's that?'

'I touched Doctor Morton when I carried her in here and put her on the bunk.'

'So you're infected?' Clancy gasped.

'I might be,' said Rory. 'I'll have to get MARVE to test me to see if I have got the virus.' He switched off the radio and looked at the robot. 'If I get ill, are you ready to take over, MARVE?'

The little robot's head bobbed up and down. 'Affirmative,' he said. Rory thought it looked as if MARVE was smiling.

Amy slowly opened her eyes. Her head hurt. A lot. It felt like someone had been playing the drums in her brain. She put a hand to her forehead and moaned as she sat up. She was no longer wearing the diving suit but was glad she still had yellow overalls on.

'Doctor?' she asked looking around her. She was startled to see that she wasn't in *The Verne* any longer. Instead she was lying on a damp, stone floor in a small cave. It was lit with some form of glowing seaweed. Amy remembered the Doctor's silly joke and she gave a small smile.

Then she saw an oval window and her smile slipped off her face. Beyond the glass was a really ugly creature. It had a wide mouth that was full of very pointy, very sharp teeth. It had two huge eyes, that were completely gold and the size of footballs. It looked like the creature was holding a giant fork. Whatever it was, it looked pointy and Amy decided she didn't want to find out if it felt as sharp as it looked.

She realised the cave must be some sort of cell and that the creature behind the glass was a guard.

'Doctor!' she called, more loudly.

A groaning noise came from behind her and Amy turned to see what was there. She was very relieved to see that the body lying there was wearing a tweed jacket. So, unless the fish creatures had taken to wearing woolly clothes, she was pretty sure it was the Doctor.

'Ooh,' the Doctor said. 'Electrical overload. Causes the body and brain to shut down.'

'They knocked us out, you mean,' Amy said, and pulled the Doctor to his feet.

'Thank you,' he said. 'Yes. That is exactly what I mean. They knocked us out. So, they don't want to kill us. At least, not yet.'

'Good,' Amy said. She was becoming impatient and wanted to go. 'So, can we just sonic the door, find the sub and get out of here?'

'Patience, Pond. We came here to speak with these creatures. They must be intelligent. They've built a cell especially for us. That fish, guard, monster, thing has a weapon. So, they have technology.' He pointed to a basin beside the door with about ten large shells hanging beside it. 'They've even managed to get some fresh water for us and provided something for us to drink from. So, they must be intelligent. Which is why they didn't kill us.'

'Yet,' said Amy.

The Doctor ignored his companion and walked past her to speak to the guard.

'Hello!' he said with his best smile. 'Are you in charge here? Can we speak to you? There seems to have been a terrible mix-up.'

The fish creature looked back at them and seemed to frown.

'I don't think he likes us,' said Amy.

'No,' said the Doctor. 'It's not that.' He stared at the guard for a few seconds and then he hit his forehead with his palm. 'Of course! Fish! Remember the Hath, Amy? Oh no, that wasn't you. . .'

'The Hath?'

'Doesn't matter. The point is that they are fish.'

'Well spotted,' said Amy.

'Fish don't talk.'

'Dur,' said Amy. 'Of course fish don't talk!'

'Well they do. Just not like you and I. The Hath had their bubbles, but the point is most fish don't make any sound. But they do communicate,' the Doctor said. 'Look at this chap. Look closely at his face, Amy.'

Amy looked. Although the creature was not pretty to look at, she stared really hard at its face. As she did so, she leaned nearer and nearer to the window. Suddenly the fish's face lit up with a flash of red.

Amy jumped back. 'It's the same type of fish-thing that attacked the submersible earlier,' she said.

'And?'

Amy looked blank for a few seconds and then she realised. 'It can change the colour of its skin!'

'Exactly!' The Doctor beamed. 'Now, normally, the TARDIS would translate any language but this is a little on the odd side. It can't help us with this. No. We need to find a way to say "hello" to Mister Angler Fish, here.'

He spun around on the spot and walked a few paces back to the corner of the cell. He had his hands clasped together and both index fingers sticking out, touching. Amy knew that he was deep in thought. Then his fingers began to wiggle. Amy knew this meant he had come up with a plan – or was about to.

'Creating colour from nothing. I mean, it's not easy, is it?' the Doctor said. ''We have your clothes. My clothes.'

'I am NOT taking my clothes off!' said Amy indignantly.

The Doctor shook his head. 'No, no, no. I just need a piece of them. A bit of your yellow boiler suit.'

'A bit? You mean you're going to cut up my overalls?' Amy looked defiantly at the Doctor. 'No way!'

'Oh, stop moaning,' the Doctor said, taking the sonic screwdriver from his pocket. 'I'll get you a new one!' The sonic screwdriver buzzed and the

Doctor quickly cut a square the size of a crisp from the side of Amy's jumper. 'There!' he said.

Then he cut a piece from her skirt and moved on to his own clothing. The sonic quickly cut a square out of his greeny-brown jacket and another from his black trousers at the ankle.

'Now we just need some way of mixing them,' he said.

'And we don't know what the colours mean,' Amy reminded him.

'Ah,' the Doctor said and stared at the little pieces of material in his hand as if they were about to tell him what each of them meant.

Just then, the cell door opened and two guards entered. They were walking on their back fins as if they were feet. One of them held his three-pronged weapon out before him, to keep the Doctor and Amy at bay. Behind them was a different fish person. He was much lighter in colour and had smaller eyes with normal, black pupils.

'I think you'd better work it out fast!' Amy squealed.

CHAPTER 6
THE LOCKED DOOR

Rory looked up from his latest patient. MARVE entered the medical bay, pushing a floating stretcher with a man on it. The new patient was moaning and had the tell-tale signs of the yellow virus showing on his skin. There were only six beds in the room and five were already occupied. This sixth person meant that the medical bay was now full. Rory didn't know what he would do if any more people got sick.

He would have to see what extra space there was nearby. He didn't really want to talk to the captain about it because their last conversation had not ended well.

After MARVE had tested him for the virus,

he was pleased to find out he wasn't infected. So he had gone to the control room to report on the virus and what he was doing to cure the crew. As well as the captain, Mister Fleming was there with two security guards. Again, Rory was surprised by how many guards there were onboard. He wasn't sure he trusted anyone on the sub and what Captain Clancy was about to say didn't change his mind.

'I'm afraid we've lost contact with your friends, the Doctor and Amy,' Clancy said.

Rory looked at her. He was concerned but not surprised. 'When?' he asked.

'If we send out a submersible, we always keep an eye on it,' Fleming said. He pointed to a screen on one of *The Ocean Explorer*'s control panels. 'Each one sends out a signal so that we can always find it. *The Verne*'s signal stopped broadcasting forty-five minutes ago.'

'What does that mean?' Rory frowned. He didn't like the sound of this.

Clancy and Fleming looked at each other.

'Well,' said Clancy. 'The best we can hope for is that there is some natural reason why we can't pick up the signal such as some kind of chemical or tidal disturbance in the water. It's rare, but it does happen.'

'Or they might have taken the sub into a cave of some sort,' Fleming said. 'If it was under the sea bed, we wouldn't be able to pick up the signal. Or if they were out of range, but that's not likely…'

'And what if they aren't underground or in a chemical cloud or whatever?' asked Rory 'Does that mean…?' he didn't want to finish the question.

Clancy came forward and put a hand on his shoulder. 'It could mean that the sub has suffered a power failure or that is has sunk or...' she hesitated. 'Or it may mean *The Verne* has been destroyed.'

Rory looked at her and shook his head. 'No,' he said. 'No. I don't believe that. The Doctor wouldn't let that happen.'

'I'm sorry,' said Fleming.

'So what do we do about it?' asked Rory. 'They

might need help!'

'I'm sorry, Rory,' Captain Clancy said. 'But we don't have time…'

'Don't have time? Are you kidding?' Rory shouted. 'That's my wife you're talking about.'

'We have a mission to complete,' Fleming said. 'It's very important and we don't have time to hang around.'

'My wife is very important,' Rory hissed. 'The Doctor is very important. Any life is,' he looked at the captain. 'If you want my help with this virus, you'd better find a way to "hang around" and look for them.'

Clancy held her hands up. 'OK, look. We'll launch a rescue buoy.'

'What good will that do?' asked Rory.

'A rescue buoy is a floating pod that has emergency food and water supplies,' Fleming explained. 'It also has a radio so the Doctor and Amy can contact us if their one is damaged. The pod can also be sealed off from the sea so it is warm and dry if they need to stay there for a while.'

'The rescue buoy will send out a signal to *The Verne*,' Clancy added. 'If the sub is damaged, and it's got any power left, the pod will bring it to the surface by auto-pilot.'

Rory nodded. He didn't believe for one second that the Doctor and Amy were dead, but if they were in trouble, he wanted to be sure that he had done everything he could do for them. 'OK,' he said. 'You'll do that now?'

'Right away,' Clancy said. 'Mister Fleming, will you make sure the buoy is launched from the Moon Pool immediately?'

'Yes, Ma'am.' He saluted and left the control room.

'Can I still depend on your support in the medical bay?' asked Clancy.

'Yes,' Rory said. 'And I think I'd better get back there.'

That had been half an hour ago.

Rory was now rushing around, giving medicine to six crewmen and hoping that it would work. It was difficult because he had run out of plastic tents and so he had to wear his biohazard suit all the time. No one else was allowed in the medical bay and only MARVE was allowed to pick up crewmen who developed the virus.

Everyone else was wearing gloves and face masks that made them all look like doctors in an operating theatre. Rory knew that they were all afraid too, because no one wanted to catch the virus.

Rory sighed. No matter what was going on elsewhere on the submarine, he had a job to do. Right now that meant looking for more room in case anyone else got sick and he had a nasty feeling that would definitely happen.

There was an uncomfortable silence in the cell. The new arrival – a far more attractive-looking fish than the two guards – was looking at the

Doctor. This was because the Doctor was miming silently, trying to say hello and introduce himself and his companion. He even tried to wave the coloured squares that he had cut from his and Amy's clothing.

'I don't think that's working,' said Amy.

'Shhh,' the Doctor held a finger to his lips. 'If they don't use sound to communicate they might find it strange or impolite if we do.'

'Tough,' said Amy.

The Doctor looked at her. 'Please, Amelia.'

'All right,' whispered Amy and she stood back to allow the Doctor to continue his efforts.

'I think I'm starting to understand some of what they're saying when they flash different colours,' the Doctor explained in a whisper. 'But I think we've got a long way to go yet.'

Makron watched the strange creatures through the cell window. He found them a little bit frightening but also a little bit funny at the same time. Makron had decided that the pink creature with the brown hair on its head was in charge and the one with the long, orange hair was its friend or helper. He also assumed that because of its bone structure and size that the one with brown hair was male.

When they started making noises at each other, Makron almost laughed. He could see his father's face, which told him that his father did not think it was funny at all. Then the one with the brown hair started using his coloured squares again.

He held up the green one first and then pointed at different things in the cell: the basin, the one with orange hair, the guard. Then he made a movement with his shoulders that made his neck look shorter. Makron had no idea what he was doing.

His father moved forward, changing the colour of his skin to ask the question, *'What are you doing here?'*

The male creature was staring at his father. Then he smiled and lifted a hand to wave his fingers around by Darkin's face. Makron could see this didn't please his father, but he stayed still. Then the male pointed to his own face and shook his head. He held up a piece of red material.

Was he saying that his face hurt? Makron wondered. Then he realised. The creature was trying to talk. He bashed the long fins of his hand on the window. Darkin and the two low swimmers turned round to look at him.

'They're trying to talk to you!' Makron said.

'What do you mean?' asked Darkin. *'Why don't they talk normally?'*

'They can't talk normally,' Makron said. *'They can't change their skin colour. The male is trying to use the cloth.'*

Darkin ordered the guards to let his son in and turned back to the prisoners. He pointed at them and flashed violet. *'You're aliens,'* he said.

The male nodded and held up the black square of material.

'He's asking you if you're in charge, I think,' Makron pulsed.

Darkin flashed his cheeks white for a second and bobbed his head. Yes.

The male clapped his hands together and started making noises to the female. Darkin's face went a little red with annoyance. The Shoal did not make sounds so they did not think it was polite for others to do so.

Makron sighed. His father didn't understand. These were aliens. Everything they did would seem odd to the Shoal. It must be the same for them.

The Doctor was smiling, his eyes narrowed with happiness.

'Ok, clever clogs,' Amy said. 'You managed to say "hello" to the fish people! Now what?'

'Now we can explain that we're friendly and they can let us go,' the Doctor said.

'I've heard that before,' Amy replied.

'Well, this time, it will work,' the Doctor said a little sadly. 'I'm sure it will.'

'Go on then,' Amy said, and waved him back to his conversation with the fish creatures.

Aboard *The Ocean Explorer*, Rory had found a short side corridor just down the main passage from the medical bay. It was narrow and not very well lit. He hesitated and then took a step forward as if the corridor floor was alarmed and if he trod too hard bells would go off all over the submarine.

Nothing happened, so he sighed with relief and nodded his head. Yeah, this would be all right. He took another step and stopped. There was a door in the wall to his right. It had a small, round window in it but there appeared to be a shutter over it on the inside. Rory stared at it.

As far as he could tell, this corridor was next to the medical bay, but the medical bay only had one door into it. So where did this door go? Rory went back to where the side corridor joined the main passageway. He walked steadily back to the medical bay door, counting his paces. It took him twelve strides. Then he went back inside the medical bay and counted his steps from the door to the far wall. It was only eight.

That couldn't be right. Unless there was another room there.

He quickly returned to the T-junction in the corridor and looked about to make sure he hadn't made a mistake. No. He had come out of the medical bay, turned right, walked down the passage and found this little corridor to the right. He frowned. I suppose I'd better check out what was behind the door, he thought. If it was another room, it would be the best place to put any extra sailors that got sick.

He dipped into his pocket and brought out Doctor Morton's security pass. He slowly reached out to put the pass on the panel beneath the door handle.

'Can I help you?'

Rory jumped and dropped the card. It was Fleming. He was standing in the main corridor looking down the side passage. He had one hand on the holster where he kept his gun.

'Sorry,' Rory said. Why did he say that? He

shook his head. 'I was, um, looking for some more space. You know, for the patients. Not space like outer space. Space like room. For extra beds.'

'Well you won't find it down there.'

'Really?' Rory asked. 'I thought this door might lead to another room. I mean, it's a bit strange but...'

Mister Fleming walked towards him. 'It's just a cupboard,' he said.

'Of course,' Rory said. 'Just a cupboard.' He held out his hand and grasped the door handle. Mister Fleming moved forward suddenly as if to stop Rory, but the door was locked.

'Locked,' said Fleming. 'As it should be.' He took Rory's hand off the door handle. 'It's a security cupboard,' he explained, dropping Rory's hand.

'Right,' Rory looked down. 'Nothing special.'

'That's right,' Fleming said with a smile. He seemed relieved that Rory understood. Then the smile faded as he saw something on the floor. The security officer bent down and picked up Doctor

Morton's security pass.

'What are you doing with this?'

'I needed it to unlock the lockers in the medical bay,' Rory explained.

'Did you now?' Fleming looked at Rory as if he was suddenly a threat. 'Are they still unlocked?'

'Yes.'

'Then you don't need this anymore, do you?'

'I suppose not,' Rory said. He was still standing by the door. Fleming beckoned him to come back to the main corridor.

Rory hesitated. Should he say this? Oh well... 'Why would you put a window in a cupboard door? And then why would you put a shutter over the window on the inside?'

Mister Fleming stepped up to Rory so that they were face to face. Rory managed not to move even though he felt scared of the other man.

'It's a security matter,' said Fleming. 'Forget about it.'

Rory nodded. 'Sure,' he said.

'Now return to the medical bay,' the security officer hissed. 'And stay there. I will see if we can find you another room for the patients. Get it?'

Rory bobbed his head again. 'I understand,' he said and walked back to the medical bay. The Doctor was right. There was something strange going on. And it had something to do with that cupboard. Mister Fleming might have taken Doctor Morton's pass but Rory had a plan to find out what was in there.

CHAPTER 7
COLOURFUL LANGUAGE!

When the Doctor was excited he looked a bit like a meerkat or a squirrel – darting about the place with bright eyes. Amy thought that if he had a tail it would definitely be bushy and twitching!

He had realised that he needed many more colours to talk to the fish creatures. He seemed to be happiest when he had to think quickly and make stuff up on the spot.

While the Doctor had been waving the bits of clothing at the fish people, Amy had been looking at the cave they were in. Its floor was sandy and when she bent to rub her fingers in the grains she could feel that it was a bit damp. The rock of the back wall was quite uneven with different types of seaweed growing in small clumps here and there.

Amy realised that the cave must usually be underwater for the seaweed to live. The fish creatures must have drained the water from it so that she and the Doctor could breathe. She hoped that whatever the Doctor was doing would work, because she didn't want to be in the cave cell if the fish people changed their minds and let the water back in.

She stood with her arms folded as the Doctor ran to the basin and grabbed the shells that they were supposed to use for drinking. He filled five of them with water and left the others empty. He put them all on the floor of the cave between him and the four fish people. Then he took out the sonic screwdriver.

Immediately, the guards moved forward with their weapons, but the fish creature in charge ordered them back. They stood by the door holding their weapons at the ready.

The Doctor didn't even seem to notice and just started waving the sonic screwdriver over all the types of seaweed that were growing on the wall. Suddenly he bent down and put the device in his mouth and plucked at one of the plants, grabbing as much as he could. Then he dashed back to the row of shells and dropped an equal amount of the plant in to the middle three.

'What on earth are you doing?' Amy asked.

'Hydron, Amy. We're on Hydron. Not Earth,' the Doctor mumbled. He still had the sonic screwdriver clenched lengthways between his teeth.

'Yup,' said Amy. 'I know where we are. Why are you running about picking seaweed?'

The Doctor looked up at her and smiled. 'It's a pH indicator,' he said.

'A what?'

'It tells you how much acid something has in it,' he explained. 'Didn't you ever do this at home?'

'Nope,' Amy wasn't impressed.

'Well on Earth you'd use red cabbage, probably. Fortunately there's some form of sea kale here that contains the same ingredient as red cabbage – it's called flavin. Anyway, if you boil it up in water, it will change colour when you add stuff to it.'

Amy smiled. He was the maddest, most brilliant person she had ever met. 'So how do you boil the water…'

Before she could finish what she was saying, the Doctor had pointed the sonic screwdriver at the first shell and had switched it on. As it buzzed away at a high pitch, the water started to bubble and then boil. Thin tufts of steam floated up towards the ceiling.

All the fish creatures were watching the Doctor, too. They seemed just as amazed and fascinated by the Doctor as Amy was. His smile got wider. The Doctor had this effect on most people.

Soon the Doctor had a row of shells with boiling water and seaweed in them. As Amy watched, the plants started to turn the water a dark pink colour.

Then he started patting his pockets and pulling all manner of things from them. He had a small ball of string, a tangerine, a stick of chalk, a handful of paperclips and a tiny sachet of tomato ketchup.

The fish creatures looked at one another.

The Doctor ignored the funny looks he was getting and quickly peeled the tangerine. He squeezed the juice from it into the farthest shell. Then he tore open the tomato ketchup and added it quickly into the nearest seashell. Finally he took the piece of chalk, broke it into pieces and added it to the middle shell. Then he whipped out the sonic screwdriver again and dipped it into the water cups, one at a time.

'Usually you'd have to wait a little bit for this to work, but we need to speak with these people quickly!'

Amy saw that the contents of the three shells were changing colour. The one with the ketchup in it became yellow, while the one with tangerine juice had gone a brilliant red. The shell with the piece of chalk in was turning a dark blue.

'So now we have three colours,' Amy said. She was still confused. 'Didn't we have three colours of material anyway?

'Watch, Pond!' The Doctor picked up the yellow and the blue. 'These three are primary colours, which means we can do this!' He poured a little of each into one of the empty shells and stood back. One shell now had green water in it. He quickly mixed purple, orange and brown. He left one shell with clear water in it.

'And the material is still useful!' The Doctor held up the square of black he had cut from her dress and then placed it into the last shell that had water in it. He applied the sonic screwdriver, which boiled the water with a buzz. In the steaming water, the black colour ran from the cotton, turning the water black, too.

'There!' the Doctor said. He stood back and admired his handiwork. He had a full rainbow of colours as well as black and clear. 'Now we can have a proper conversation!'

On *The Ocean Explorer,* Rory was feeling very pleased with himself. When Mister Fleming had taken Doctor Morton's security pass, he had known exactly where to get another one. One of the patients that had been brought into the medical bay earlier was a security guard. Not only was Rory pleased with himself for realising that the security guard would have a pass, he was also happy because he had worked out that a security guard could go anywhere.

While MARVE was looking after one of the other sick crewmen, Rory moved over to where the security guard was sleeping. He checked that the robot wasn't watching and then searched the man's pockets for the pass. Sure enough he found it in the left-hand jacket pocket. Rory quickly slipped the pass into his own pocket and then told the robot he was going to the toilet.

He walked out into the corridor and along it for a few metres to where the passage was. He quickly walked up to the door with the round window in it. He pressed the security pass against the panel under the handle and pulled the door open.

Beyond the door the room was dark, but Rory could see it was bigger than a cupboard. The room had two rows of large, glass tubes that looked a little like the one on top of the TARDIS control console. They were about the width of a dustbin and were full of water. A strange blue light lit up these tubes from underneath, and inside each Rory could see there was a dark circle the size of a football.

Rory stepped into the room and moved to look at the nearest tube. Small bubbles were coming from the bottom of the cylinder as if the water inside was being kept full of air – like a pump does in a fish tank. He stared at the dark footballs and wondered what they could be. Then he caught sight of a shape against the light. There was something inside the football.

He moved back to the door and hunted about for a light switch. As he did so, he saw a work bench against the far wall. On the bench, lit up by a single spotlight, was a large plastic container. Rory frowned. Why was it under a spotlight? It must be important, he thought, so he went over to take a look at that instead. As he got closer he thought he could smell something and when he took the lid off the plastic box he could see why. The stink of fish was over-powering and he had to put a hand over his nose and mouth to stop himself being sick.

Slowly, he looked into the box. At first he thought it was actually seaweed, not an animal. Whatever it was, it must have been rotting. Yuck! Rory looked away again. Then he told himself it was OK. He plucked up the courage and took another look.

It was just a lump of stuff, like a flap of skin – in fact just like a deflated, black football, only more slimy. Then he realised what it was. The things in the tubes were the baby fish. Rory turned round and looked at the glowing glass containers. The dark shapes hanging in each one were not balls. They were fish eggs!

Rory knew there was a special word for fish eggs. He scratched his chin as he thought. Fish roe! That was it! Then his hand fell away from his face. Roe. That was what Doctor Morton had been saying! Not Row! The two words sounded the same but she must have been talking about the fish eggs. Now he thought about it, the room was right next to the medical bay.

So she was trying to warn him about the fish eggs. But why? And the thing in the box, wasn't really the whole egg. It was just the outer covering. Not a shell, because fish eggs didn't have shells like birds' eggs did. It was more like a case or a seed pod.

Rory wondered why they were there. The submarine had only just arrived on the planet and no one had been outside the ship except Amy and the Doctor. And why was Mister Fleming so keen to hide the eggs from Rory? Were they going to let the eggs out into the sea on Hydron? Was it like returning captive animals to the wild or something? There was only one way to find out. Rory would have to ask the captain.

Rory marched away from the workbench and out into the passage. He pushed the door shut and had just turned round again when all the lights on the submarine went out. The power had gone. Then he noticed that not only was there no light, but the air pumps had stopped working. They'd suffocate! The darkened sub lurched suddenly and Rory realised he was wrong. They wouldn't suffocate. They'd never get the chance! The submarine had no power. It was sinking – and fast...

CHAPTER 8
THE WATER VOLCANO

Rory stumbled out into the passage and hit his head against the metal wall. An alarm was sounding and red emergency lights had come on. The submarine was bathed in the strange crimson glow, making it look like a small area of hell. Rory checked his head but it wasn't bleeding. He'd live. Then he closed the door to the small lab with the tubes in it and lurched into the main corridor.

The Ocean Explorer swayed violently to one side, again sending Rory falling against a bulkhead wall. At the same time a rushing noise, like a leaf blower or a really big fan, filled the ship. Rory was sitting on the deck now so the next movement didn't affect him so much. Again, the submarine tipped to one side at an angle.

Rory had to find out what was going on.

He stood up carefully and stretched out his arms so that he was pressing against both sides of the corridor. Then he started walking, using his arms to brace against any sudden movement. He reached the meeting area behind the control room and stepped through the hatch that led from the corridor. Then he noticed that the whole ship was angled up. They were surfacing.

Captain Clancy gripped the leather command chair arms very tightly. Everyone was watching the depth gauge which seemed to be working despite the power failure. Rory could see it ticking quite quickly towards zero.

Rory reached the captain's chair. 'What happened?' he asked.

Clancy didn't look at him. 'I don't know,' she replied quietly. She was watching the digital display that showed their depth even more closely. It now read 24, 23, 22…

'We lost power across the ship. Our engines just stopped working. Luckily we've got a small backup generator.' Finally she looked at him. 'That gave us the power to blow the ballast tanks so that the sub could surface. I just hope we blew enough air into them to reach sea level.'

'Blow the tanks?' he asked. The depth gauge read 14, 13, 12…

'The *Ocean Explorer* is just a metal tube full of air, really,' Captain Clancy said. 'To go underwater, the submarine has to make itself heavier. So we have special tanks that can be filled with water to go down and then "blown" full of air, which pushes the water out and makes the submarine go up.'

'Right,' Rory said. He looked back at the digital readout. 5, 4, 3…

'Looks like we made it!' Clancy jumped from her chair, took some binoculars from a junior crewman and ran towards a hatch at the back of the control room.

'Where are you going?' asked Rory.

'Up top. For a look. You coming?'

'Sure!' Rory followed her to the hatch and up a ladder to another level.

There was another hatch, this time above their heads. Clancy started turning the small wheel on the hatch to open it. Then she pushed up with a grunt of effort and the door swung open, letting a shower of water in. Rory jumped back, but Clancy ignored it and climbed the last ladder out onto the top of the submarine's tower.

Rory emerged from the hatch onto a slippery metal deck about the size of a double bed. It was just wide enough for Clancy and him to stand side by side. She was leaning on the low, metal wall that ran all the way round the top of the tower. There was a gap at the back of the wall where a ladder ran down from the top of the tower, down to the main part of the outside deck.

'There!' said the captain, pointing. Even without binoculars, Rory could see that there was an island ahead of them. He guessed it might be about ten miles away. He wasn't very good with distances.

'I thought there wasn't any land on this planet,' he said. 'You know, you said it was a water world…'

'There are islands,' she replied. 'But they're more like steep mountains sticking out of the sea. You can't build anything on them. You'll see.'

'Will I?' Rory asked.

'Yes. We're going to that island. That's where the company wants us to go. So that's where we're going.'

'But what's there?' Rory asked.

'My report says there is a mineral in the lake that we can use for power.'

'But we don't have any power right now,' Rory argued.

'We've got enough to get us there.'

'And then what?'

'Then, we'll see, won't we?'

In the cell, the Doctor seemed to be making progress. He was slowly learning what the colours that he had in each shell might mean. He had taken off his jacket and was sitting with his legs crossed on the sandy floor.

'The fish people have a very complicated way of talking!' Amy said. 'Won't it take forever just to say one sentence?'

The Doctor shook his head. 'They're not fish people, Amy,' he said as he smiled at the group in front of him. 'As far as I can understand, they are called 'the Shoal'.

'"The Shoal"?'

'Yes. It means a group of fish. Like a herd of cows or a flock of birds,' the Doctor paused for effect. 'A shoal of fish. He pointed to his most recent addition to the shells. It had diluted black water in it. 'That's grey, by the way. Grey means "together" or "group", as well as "strength". I think. Anyway I am guessing they call themselves the Shoal and that an individual is a Shoaly or

Shoalite. Shoaly, I think.'

Amy frowned. 'It doesn't sound very clear to me,' she said.

'It's not,' the Doctor grinned. 'Like you say, it's very complex. When they use colour they sometimes move their cheek fins at the same time.' His grin faded. 'I can't do that.'

'Aww, poor Doctor,' Amy joked. 'Can't move his cheek fins!' she laughed.

The Shoalys stared at Amy. The Doctor shushed her.

'Don't make silly noises, Amy,' the Doctor hissed. 'Remember? They think it's rude.'

Amy pouted her lips. 'So does your colourful water display mean you can tell them we aren't baddies and that they can let us go?'

'I'm working on it,' the Doctor said and he returned his attention to the Shoal.

He pointed at the blue and then the yellow.

'Are you trying to tell them how to make green?' Amy asked with an eyebrow raised.

'Amelia!' The Doctor sighed. 'Very well. I will explain it to you. I am saying "peaceful" and then "friend". I hope.'

The larger of the two Shoaly that looked like a lion fish turned his cheek blue and then yellow in reply.

'There! You see?' The Doctor smiled again.

'Oh yeah!' Amy was impressed. 'Can you ask them for a cup of tea?'

'One step at a time,' the Doctor said. 'We have to take care. If I point at the wrong colour I might offend them.'

'You mean... naughty words in fish language?' she giggled.

The Doctor ignored this and started pointing at the shells again, explaining what he hoped he was saying to the Shoal.

The wind ruffled Rory's hair as he leaned on the tower's handrail. *The Ocean Explorer* had taken about an hour to cover the twelve miles to the island. In the meantime, Rory had met with Mister Fleming. The security officer had shown him a spare bunk room that he could use for any extra patients. This was lucky, because two more crew had come in with signs of the yellow virus.

Rory had decided not to say anything about the strange fish roe he had found in the lab behind the medical bay. He thought that Fleming would probably lock him up – or worse – if Rory told anyone what he knew. He now knew that Fleming and Morton were in it and he wondered if Captain Clancy was in on it too, but he would have to wait to find out.

Once Rory had given the new patients the medicine to help them sleep, there wasn't much more he could do for them. He hoped that by sleeping, the sick crewmen would be able to fight off the virus. MARVE was now monitoring their life signs to make sure they didn't get worse. So far, none of them had. But they didn't show any sign of getting better either. Rory was just a nurse. What he really needed was a doctor. Or better still, *the* Doctor!

Ahead of him now, Rory could see the huge mountain of the island. It was massive. It towered into the purple clouds like a skyscraper – thousands of metres high. He couldn't see the top because it was so high it was in the clouds. The sides of the mountain rose almost vertically from the ocean, like cliffs. Whatever that satellite report had said, it was right about one thing: there was no way of building anything on it. There was no flat land at all.

'Having fun, Mister Williams?'

Rory looked round. It was Captain Clancy. He smiled. 'Tell me again. Why have we come here?' he asked.

The captain explained that before her team had come to Hydron, she had read the report on the planet. She had learned about the islands and that – amazingly – there was a lake at the top of each mountain.

'A lake?'

'Yes. We think that the islands are water volcanoes,' Clancy said. 'On each island, the lake at the top is linked to the sea below by a network of underground tunnels. The water flows down from the lake through these tunnels.'

'So how does the water get up there in the first place?'

'In the same way water gets about on Earth – it rains,' Captain Clancy pointed at the purple clouds.

'So the lake is fresh water?'

'Yes,' Clancy smiled. 'But that's not why we are here. The report says that we can use something in the lake as fuel for our engines.'

As she spoke, the submarine entered the shadow cast by the huge volcano and Rory shivered because of the slight temperature drop.

'But how do we get up there?' Rory asked.

'We climb.'

CHAPTER 9
ADMIRAL ICKTHEUS

A short distance from the Assembly building in Reef was a darker, more forbidding one. It was carved from grey coral rather than the orange of the other structures. Bright red seaweed floated from its roofs and towers. This told every member of the Shoal that this was the base of the low swimmers.

The low swimmers had always been the guardians of the Shoal. No other swimmer was allowed to join their ranks. Only the low swimmers with their bigger bodies and electrical lure – the glowing balls of skin that hung down from their foreheads – were strong enough to get through the very tough training and pass the tests that allowed them to join the Shoal Navy.

The Shoal Navy supplied all the police for Hydron's cities and all its soldiers. Every Assembly guard was a low swimmer. They had been doing the same job for hundreds of years. They had their own traditions of celebrating ancient battle and honours won.

Their history was something that the highest ranking officer in the Shoal Navy was very proud of. His name was Admiral Icktheus and he was one of the largest low swimmers on the planet. His office was in the basement of the building where there was almost no light. Because the low swimmers had evolved at greater depths than the other members of the Shoal, they preferred it dark.

At this moment, Admiral Icktheus was floating in his office behind a stone desk wearing what looked like sunglasses. The darkened lenses shielded his bulging, golden eyes from the light that came in through the gaps in the branches. He hated the light. He wished he could live in the deeper Pools of the ocean, but because he was so important he had to be in the capital city.

Admiral Icktheus was in charge of the safety and defence of the Shoal. He had been told about the aliens and their submarine as soon as Makron had told Darkin. There had been a meeting of the Assembly and Icktheus had said they should destroy the invaders right away. The Governors did not like that idea. They wanted to see if the visitors would be friendly.

Icktheus shook his head slowly. They were mad. They knew that these "humans" were there to hurt them. Why did they pretend that this was not the case? But his plan had not been accepted. He was told that he needed to come up with a new idea. So he had chosen one very good soldier to get onboard the submarine and give them a virus.

He had wanted the virus to be deadly. He wanted to wipe out the humans on the submarine. But, again, the Governors had refused him. Instead, they just wanted to make the humans sick, not to kill them. Icktheus already knew humans and so he had sent his low swimmer with a "friendly" – yellow – virus.

However, making the humans ill had not slowed them down. Icktheus was shocked to discover that the submarine was still heading for one of the Founts. Shock had turned to anger when he realised which Fount they were trying to reach.

Without checking with the Assembly, the Admiral had ordered his marine commandos to stop the submarine. He knew that the Governors would be weak. He knew they would ask him not to hurt the humans, so that is what he had told his soldiers. For the moment, anyway.

Now, he was waiting for an update on how that attack had gone. He hoped it had been successful. He reached into a small cage on his desk and pulled out a small creature that looked like a sea snail. He popped it into his mouth and chewed it with a revolting crunching sound. Ooze from the snail's body dribbled down his chin and he wiped it away with a thick fin on his flipper.

One of his junior officers appeared at the curtain of seaweed that hung over the office door.

He pulsed the colour of turquoise. *'May I come in, Sir?'* he asked.

A white flash from Icktheus told the young Shoaly he could enter. The smaller fish darted inside and knelt on his front and back flippers. Then he stood up and began his report.

The submarine had been attacked as the admiral had ordered. The engines had been knocked out, forcing the humans to take their strange ship to the surface for air. Icktheus smiled at this, glowing yellow with satisfaction. The young officer hesitated.

'What?' demanded the admiral. Something had gone wrong.

The low swimmer attack squad had used a power drain creature called a Black-Trout on the submarine and the ship had been forced to surface. However, the humans had a backup engine. The Black-Trout did not work on this new engine because the power source the motor used was not the same.

'Are you telling me they use two types of fuel?' Admiral Icktheus asked.

'Yes, Sir.'

'And?'

Again the officer hesitated. 'The submarine has reached the Fount, Sir.'

'What?' the admiral made a growling noise. This shocked the other Shoaly. Icktheus managed to control his temper. 'What are the humans doing now?' he asked.

'We think they are trying to get to the spawning pool, Sir.'

This time Admiral Icktheus could not control himself. He burst from behind his desk, glowing red all over. He came face to face with the young Shoaly and slowly took off his sunglasses.

'Summon my personal squadron,' he said. 'I will deal with this myself.'

The Ocean Explorer was nestled in the shadow of the huge mountain. Thick cables had been attached to the submarine and tied to the island using metal loops that had been hammered into the rock. A gangway had been set up between the side hatch in the submarine's tower and the cliff.

On the deck of the sub, two crewmen in blue overalls were attaching ropes to the end of a special climbing gun. It looked like a harpoon gun and had a big spike sticking out of it. According to Captain Clancy, using this gun would mean the climb would be much quicker. If they started out from sea level, it could take them over two days to climb the mountain.

The gun would shoot the great big spike into the rock as high as it could reach. Then, a winch would pull one climber at a time to where the spike was. Because the winch was fast, it would mean that they could go up by several hundred metres in less than an hour.

Because the winch could only be used with the

harpoon gun and that was too big to take up the mountain, they would then have to climb the rest from there, which should take about six hours the captain reckoned.

Rory looked away from the climbing gun and lifted his head to gaze up at the mountain soaring over his head. Was he really going to climb this thing? He was now dressed in blue overalls which were fitted with a climbing harness. This climbing harness reminded Rory of a kind of strange pair of Y-front pants.

Captain Clancy came to stand beside him. 'It's easy, really,' she said.

'Really?' Rory asked. He wasn't so sure.

Then the last member of the ascent team joined them. He was their leader because he was the most experienced climber.

'Ready?' asked Mister Fleming.

'As I'll ever be,' Rory replied.

'Let's do this!' said the captain.

CHAPTER 10
THE STAGNANT POOL

The Doctor stood with his hands clasped behind his back. Amy was amazed. He'd done it. He was actually talking to the Shoal and they were talking back to him and everyone seemed to understand each other. Except Amy. She sort of understood what was going on and had learned vaguely what the colours meant, but every colour seemed to have a hundred meanings and the Doctor was doing a brilliant job of working out what they meant.

A whole group of the Shoal that looked like lion fish were gathered in the room and two colourful fish were holding the Doctor's and Amy's diving suits.

'Are they letting us go?' Amy asked.

'Not exactly,' the Doctor said. 'It seems they want to show us their city. I think they want me to speak to their government or committee or assembly. I haven't quite worked out which word is the best translation.'

'You're going to speak to their leaders with a nursery school activity pack?' Amy asked pointing at the row of shells with coloured water in them.

'Obviously we can't take that with us,' the Doctor said. 'I have asked for some bits and bobs so I can make a portable translator. I imagine it will look a bit like a Christmas decoration, but it'll come in useful when we get a tree for next year.'

They looked at one another. After the last Christmas adventure they'd had, Amy hoped that having a tree in the TARDIS would be a simple way of staying out of trouble. But she doubted it.

'So now what? Who are the bright fish people?'

The Doctor pursed his lips. 'They are medium swimmers. They're the general workforce. The guards are low swimmers. The military, basically. The other, stripy fellows are the high swimmers. They're in charge.'

'High rollers, more like,' Amy said.

'Well. Exactly. But please try to remember: they're Shoal not "fish people".'

'Right,' Amy said. 'Totally different.'

'Actually they are. Very different,' the Doctor replied. 'The fish people lived in Atlantis and they looked more like people than fish.'

Amy looked at him. Then she shook her head. 'Anyway…'

'The leader of the Shoal is this one here. I think his name sounds like "darkness", but I'm not sure,' the Doctor frowned at his lack of knowledge. 'He says we will be taken to a place where I can make a translation machine.'

'And then we get the grand tour?'

'Yes,' the Doctor said with a smile. 'I'm rather looking forward to that. It's been a while since I saw an underwater city.'

There were blisters starting to form on Rory's hands. Since they had left the "base" that the gun had managed to shoot to, the climb was slow and dangerous. And now it was painful, even though he was wearing gloves. They had been climbing for almost five hours. Each time they moved up the mountain, Rory had to grip the rope and pull. If he could, he used whatever footholds he could find on the cliff to push himself up at the same time.

The air was thinner at this height too, and it was more difficult to breathe. An hour or so ago, they had entered a layer of thick, foggy cloud and Rory could hardly see a thing. He was exhausted and beginning to wish he hadn't come.

Above him Mister Fleming was flat against the cliff face hammering a device called a piton into a small crack in the rock. He then attached the rope they were all using as a guide to the end sticking out and made his next move up the cliff, slowly feeling for any handholds.

'Are we there yet?' Rory asked. He was only half joking.

'Save your breath for climbing,' Fleming replied. Even he was puffing with effort.

'I'd like an answer to that question as well,' Captain Clancy said. She was just below Rory, clinging to the wall of stone as if her life depended on it. Which it did.

'All right,' Fleming stopped moving and looked down at them. 'We are almost there, actually. According to the scanner, we should crest the top in about ten minutes.'

'Keep going, then' Clancy called. Fleming nodded and set off into the mist like a cautious spider.

Rory pressed his helmeted head against the rock. Then he took a deep breath and started climbing again. He began to wonder how they would get down. Wasn't it easier to climb up something than get down again? Or was that just cats in trees?

While he was thinking this, Fleming reached the top and gave a whoop of joy! Rory sped up and emerged through the mist into bright sunshine. He scrambled over the edge of the cliff and then turned to help Captain Jane. She smiled at him as he pulled her onto the summit. Then they stood up and joined Mister Fleming who was staring at the sight before them.

Just like the captain had said, the water volcano had a lake in a crater on the top of it. It had a thin rim on which the three of them were standing, that sloped to the water's edge. The sky seemed less purple at this height – more mauve or violet than the deep purple it appeared on the surface.

Of course, Rory realised that just like on Earth, the water on Hydron wasn't the same colour as the sky. The water just reflected the colour of the sky above. Because the sky was purple that is what colour the sea looked.

Rory had imagined that the pool would be beautiful and crystal clear. After all, it was supposed to be pure water, wasn't it? However, it was anything but. The water was a dark brown colour and it had an oily film on its surface. Rory wrinkled his nose. There was an unpleasant smell, like mouldy socks – and it seemed familiar.

'I wouldn't exactly tell my friends to come here on holiday,' Rory said.

'Nor would I,' the captain replied. She took off her helmet and walked towards the lake. 'What could possibly be in here that can power our reactor engines?' she asked.

'The report said that there were power readings in the water,' Fleming said. Rory thought he sounded like a bad actor that had forgotten to learn his lines and was making it up as he went along. 'Perhaps some form of mineral? Uranium? I don't know…'

Rory stepped towards the stagnant pool and stared down into its depths. It was only then that he started to see the shapes in the water. Because the liquid was dark – and thick with some nasty substance – he couldn't quite make out what they were.

'Have you got a torch or something we can put in the water and see what those are?' he asked.

Fleming unhooked something from his belt and handed it to Rory. 'It's a diver's flashlight,' he said.

'Thanks,' Rory took the torch and turned it on, holding it underwater so that he could see what the shapes were. Suddenly he stumbled back. He now realised why he recognised the smell. It was the same one he'd smelled in the lab on the submarine. 'No,' he said. 'It can't be.'

'What?' Fleming was by his side in an instant, a deep frown on his face.

'They're fish roe,' Rory said. 'Fish eggs! Well, the pods of the fish eggs, anyway. The same as the one you've been hiding in that secret room; the same as the one in the box!'

Fleming glared at Rory and then glanced at Captain Clancy. She lifted her head from the water and looked at her security officer.

'What does he mean?' she asked. 'What fish eggs? What secret room?' Her voice was becoming louder. 'Explain yourself, Mister Fleming!' she shouted.

Fleming shook his head and slowly pulled his gun from its holster. 'Sorry, Captain,' he said, 'but you don't know the whole story.'

CHAPTER 11
THE LOW SWIMMERS TAKE OVER

The undersea cave was huge. Admiral Icktheus stood in front of a dozen rows of his best commandos. There were over one hundred low swimmers in full battle kit. Each had squid grenades hanging from their belts along with their forked electric weapons. Some teams had the Black-Trout fish that looked like slugs, but were the size of elephants.

Icktheus was so angry about the humans that he decided he was going to stop them once and for all. They were going to the Fount and that was somewhere they shouldn't be going. It was against the law and against everything the Shoal believed in for anyone but a Shoaly to visit the Founts.

This was the force Icktheus was going to use to sink the submarine – just like he'd done with the last one. Only this time he was going to kill all the humans.

He was about to issue the order when one of his most trusted spies arrived. Icktheus could see him talking with one of the guards on the cave entrance. Because he had given the order that no one was to be allowed in, they weren't going to let him pass. The admiral tore himself away from the troops and swam quickly to the group. He dismissed the guards and watched as the spy delivered his message.

'I have heard something unbelievable,' the spy said. *'Some time ago, a group of low swimmers caught a small submarine with two humans aboard.'*

The stripes on Admiral Icktheus's face slowly turned from their usual black to a deep red. *'Why didn't I hear about this?'*

'The low swimmers that caught them have been kept in the rooms by the Assembly members,' the spy

reported calmly. *'Apparently they feared that you would react badly...'*

'And they were right!' Icktheus could not help himself. The growl came from deep in his throat and built to a roar that echoed through the water. Even his hardened troops stared at the admiral.

'I cannot allow this to happen,' he said. *'We have a proud tradition of defending our people from any and all threats we have faced! And now we are imprisoned and kept quiet because they do not want us to do our job properly?'*

He turned and swam back to the waiting commandos.

'First two squads! Come with me now! There are aliens in the city!'

The Doctor and Amy were once again wearing the orange diving suits from *The Verne*. They had been given them by the Shoal and had quickly put them on.

'The leader says we're going to a laboratory,'

the Doctor explained. 'Once we go out into the corridor, they'll flood the place again and then we can swim.'

They were led into the corridor and the cell door closed. Then water flooded in through pipes in the wall. At last the passage was completely submersed and another door opened and they were ushered through.

The Doctor activated his radio and spoke to Amy. 'I think this is some sort of military or police building.'

'Why do you think that?'

'Well, you don't find cells in normal houses, do you? Well, not most normal houses.'

Amy nodded. She had to agree with that.

After swimming down two more corridors, they entered a large room that was full of strange equipment and tools.

'Brilliant!' the Doctor said. 'Look at all this stuff. I love stuff. You can do all sorts of stuff with stuff.'

He quickly set about building what Amy thought of as his flashy light communicator thing. It had a rainbow of lights on it as well as a camera and a micro-computer, a speaker and a microphone.

'I've programmed the computer with what I've learned from our coloured water experiments,' the Doctor explained. 'The translator will film the Shoal and translate via the speaker unit. We can then talk to them by speaking into the microphone and the machine will then flash the correct lights so the Shoal can understand us.'

The Doctor told the guards that he had finished and the Shoal leader then arrived. He flashed in various colours and the translator relayed his words back to Amy and the Doctor in English.

'We are going to address the Assembly,' he said. 'Please come with me. We will be travelling through our capital city, Reef.'

Inside his diving helmet, Amy could see the Doctor grin.

Then, they swam to an exit where there was a large grey creature resting on the sea bed. It looked like some kind of whale. Amy was quite alarmed when it opened its massive mouth and two of the Shoal swam inside and rested against the creature's teeth, standing on what she guessed was its tongue! Amy pulled a face and stepped back. Not the Doctor. Oh, no. He just stepped right up and climbed inside!

At first Amy was not at all keen to get inside the whale. Not after the last one! She shivered as she remembered *Starship UK* and being in the belly of the Star Whale. And she knew that you didn't escape without a lot of fuss and probably some whale sick...

The amazing thing was that although the whale looked grey from out there, inside you could see through its skin. It was like tinted glass windows in a car. The animal rose from the sand and started swimming. There were two low swimmers moving along beside the whale in what looked like metal armour. Amy was reminded of the US President's limo driving through the streets with a police motorcycle escort.

As the whale made its way through the city, Amy looked out through the transparent skin. She thought that Reef was beautiful. There was so much colour and life here. It was like Piccadilly Circus in London or Times Square in New York. There were so many creatures going about their lives and all the seaweed and coral made it look really mind-blowing. She could see why the Doctor had smiled at the thought of exploring this place and she couldn't help doing the same.

The Doctor was chatting to the Shoal's leader. His machine translated whatever he said into the flashing lights and she guessed the Doctor had already picked up the Shoal language so he could understand what they were saying. It was a bit like listening to a friend on a mobile phone.

He had managed to work out the Shoal's individual names, too. He leant over to Amy. 'The leader of the Shoal is called Darkin and the younger Shoaly is his son. His name is Makron.'

Finally they slowed down as the whale

approached a large, round orange building with seaweed all over its roof.

'So that's your Assembly building?' the Doctor asked. 'Look, Amy!'

Amy looked. It looked like a pineapple to her. A pineapple under the sea! She laughed. 'Spongebob!' she said.

The Doctor frowned. 'What are you talking about, Pond?'

Amy shook her head. 'Never mind,' she said. Then she realised that she might have been a bit rude to the Shoal. 'It looks very nice.' She smiled warmly at Makron whose skin flushed a light pink colour. Perhaps he was blushing? Amy doubted it.

The whale creature came to a stop in a large alcove below the Assembly building. Amy swam out of the whale's mouth and straight into the orange corridors of the Assembly building. The Doctor followed her with Darkin and Makron. The guards had vanished, but Amy supposed they must be trusted now. The Doctor had that effect on people.

As they emerged into a bigger entrance hall, the ugliest fish Amy had ever seen swam up to them, surrounded by twenty more low swimmers. They all had their forked weapons out and were not just pointing them at Amy and the Doctor but also at Makron and Darkin.

The Doctor grimaced as the ugly fish and Darkin pulsed and flashed at each other. He turned to Amy and whispered, 'Oh dear. I think this is not going to end well. This chap's an admiral and he is saying that the Assembly have betrayed him. That we are aliens and that we are dangerous.'

'Well that's not true!' Amy said. This attracted the attention of Admiral Ugly. He swam right up to her and touched her diving helmet with his glowing green lure. There was a sizzle of electricity and Amy felt that the world was swimming – not her. She watched in a daze as the Doctor stepped up to the big fish and started talking to him very loudly.

Then she fainted and the world went black.

CHAPTER 12
THE SECRET OF THE SHOAL

Rory looked at the gun Fleming was holding. Was he serious? Rory had never really liked him but what was he doing? To be honest, Rory didn't understand and, it seemed, neither did Captain Clancy.

'So tell me! What is going on here?' she shouted.

Fleming smiled. 'You were told that we've never been to this planet before, weren't you?'

'Yes.' Clancy looked confused.

'That's not quite true,' Fleming said. 'I have been to this planet before. I came here two years ago with another team.' He stopped smiling. 'Things went wrong.'

Rory looked at the security officer and suddenly he knew what had happened. 'You came here and you took some of those creatures' eggs. And now they're angry. That's why they're attacking us.'

'We… we didn't know they were intelligent,' Fleming said. 'At first we just thought they were animals.' He paused. 'They *are* animals!' he said. 'Now, get on the radio, Captain. We need to haul a pump up here with a long enough pipe to reach back to the sub.'

'But why?' Clancy looked at Fleming. She had tears in her eyes. Rory felt both angry and sick at the same time.

'It's what the eggs are made of,' Fleming said. 'When they decompose they create amazing amounts of power. I've never seen anything like it. We tested them aboard the old submarine. *The Marine Adventurer,* it was called.' He laughed a bitter laugh. 'Some adventure. They all died. Except me and Angela Morton.'

'But what do you need them for?' Clancy asked.

'We've got all sorts of fuel. We don't need this...' She waved a hand at the polluted lake.

'You don't understand,' Fleming said. 'Just one of these things could power a starship for a week. It would make anyone a fortune.'

'So you poisoned the water here?' asked Rory through gritted teeth. 'This is where those fish grow up. This is their nursery.'

Fleming pointed his gun at Rory. 'Stay back, nursemaid!' he said. Then he turned to Clancy. 'I said, get on the radio, Captain. Do it!'

While Clancy radioed *The Ocean Explorer*, Fleming made Rory sit on the ground in front of the lake. The security officer bent down to put a pair of handcuffs on him and stood up again.

'I'll need to take these off to climb back down,' Rory pointed out.

'Who says you're going back down?'

Amy awoke to find that she was back on the sandy floor of the cell. She was still wearing the orange diving suit, but her helmet was gone. She lifted her head and brushed off a patch of sand that had stuck to her face. Then she looked round the familiar cell. The Doctor was standing by the door. Amy could just see a low swimmer through the glass window.

'What happened?' she asked.

'The admiral took a dislike to you,' the Doctor said, coming over to squat next to Amy. He placed his hand gently on her forehead, then he pulled down the eyelid on her left eye and stared at it. Finally he stuck his tongue out. Amy did the same. 'Good.' The Doctor stood up.

'Admiral?' asked Amy. 'What did he do, though?'

'He stunned you with his lure – the special type of fin that sticks out from a low swimmer's head.'

'The green, glowing thing?'

The Doctor nodded. 'And he's an admiral, yes. Admiral Icktheus: the most senior officer in the Shoal's Navy. He's taken over. We're all prisoners. Me, you, Darkin and most of the other Governors, too. Makron managed to get away.'

'After all our work?' she cried. 'We'll never get away now!'

'We will get away. We must.' The Doctor lowered his voice. 'If we don't, the admiral is going to execute us.'

'If he wants us dead, why are we in a cell?' Amy was angry now.

'He wants a public execution – he wants to show everyone that we are bad aliens and that he is doing a good job.'

'And I presume your coloured light machine won't get us out of this?'

'I think not,' the Doctor whispered. 'But I do still have this!' He showed Amy that he was holding the sonic screwdriver in his right hand.

'Great. So what are we waiting for? Let's get out of here!' She stood up and came over to the door.

'It's not that easy,' the Doctor said. 'There is a large low swimmer out there armed with a very nasty looking fork.'

As he spoke the very large low swimmer suddenly fell back against the window and slid down it until his head vanished from view. A few seconds later, Makron's face appeared. He was waving his owned pronged weapon and had the Doctor's translation device in his other hand.

The Doctor grinned and immediately pointed the sonic screwdriver at the door. After a few seconds' buzzing, the lock clicked open and the Doctor and Amy hurried out of the cell, stepping over the sleeping body of the low swimmer. Makron passed the translator to the Doctor and they quickly started talking.

'You need to come with me. Now!' Makron said via the translator.

They ran down the short corridor in the opposite direction they had taken earlier. Another low swimmer was lying on the floor. Amy guessed Makron must have already knocked him out. In the wall was a stone door. As the Shoaly pressed a button, it slid back to reveal what looked like a cupboard. Then she saw that there was another door opposite her.

'What's this?' she asked.

'Waterlock,' the Doctor replied. He took her arm and guided her inside the small chamber. 'Like an airlock, but for water.'

Amy looked at him and shrugged. 'What does that mean?'

Makron had now joined them in the tiny room and the first door was closing.

'It means that when that door closes, the chamber will fill with water,' the machine translated. 'Then the second door will open and we'll be able to swim out.'

'But we haven't got our helmets! We'll drown!' exclaimed Amy. Then she squealed as she noticed that water was already lapping at her ankles and rising fast.

'Don't worry!' the Doctor said, pinching his nose. 'Just hold your breath!'

Before Amy could ask another question, the

water level had reached her neck and she took a huge gulp of air before the water finally rose above her head, filling the room. Then, the second door opened.

Looking through water without goggles was like looking at a photo that was out of focus. Everything was hazy, but Amy could definitely see that beyond the door was a larger area with a line of bright lights set into the walls. They were all shining on a big, yellow object floating in the middle of the space.

The Doctor tugged at her sleeve and they started swimming towards the large, yellow blob. As they got nearer, Amy realised that it was *The Verne*, the little submersible they had taken from *The Ocean Explorer*. The Doctor helped her in to the airlock on top of the sub and closed the hatch on her. Amy was now bursting to breathe. Her cheeks were puffed out and she needed air urgently. Just when she thought she couldn't bear it any more, the water in the airlock was sucked away and she gasped in big mouthfuls of air.

Then she remembered that the Doctor was waiting in the water. Quickly, she undid the lock on the inner door and climbed down into *The Verne*'s cockpit. Her diving suit was full of water but she ignored the discomfort. Instead, she slammed the hatch shut and spun the handle that locked it.

Amy listened as the Doctor opened the outer hatch with a dull thud. This was followed by another thud as he closed it, and then a hissing sound as the airlock drained the water away. Then the handle on the inner hatch turned and the Doctor climbed down.

He looked fine. Amy was still breathing hard, grateful for the oxygen. The Doctor looked like he'd just come in out of a heavy rain shower. He smiled and closed the little round door again.

'Can we get out of here now?' Amy slumped into one of the pilot's chairs.

'Don't forget about Makron.' The Doctor waited for the airlock to go through its process and then the Shoaly was in the small cockpit with them. It was quite cramped, but soon the three of them were arranged comfortably: the Doctor and Amy in the pilots' seats and Makron crouched behind them.

'Hang on,' said Amy. 'Fish. Sorry. Shoalys. How do you survive out of water? I thought that sea creatures die out of water?'

'Most do,' Makron said. 'We are more advanced than most fish. We can live in air for several hours.'

'Very useful,' the Doctor said. 'Now let's go!'

He pressed the starter button on the control panel before him. *The Verne* gave a small jerk and then started motoring away from the brightly-lit area, down a dark tunnel.

CHAPTER 13
THE VERNE ESCAPES

The pump at the top of the water volcano was making a noise like a dentist's suction tube. Fleming had forced Captain Clancy and Rory to lower two thick cables from the cliff edge to the submarine below. Then the security officer had made them pull the lines back up. It was very hard work and they were both sweating a lot by the time the equipment appeared over the rim of the crater.

Fleming set up the machinery while Clancy and Rory lowered the cables again, this time to bring up the thick pipe that would take the discarded egg sacks down to the engines of *The Ocean Explorer*.

'What are you going to do when you've refuelled the sub?' asked Rory.

'Be quiet,' Fleming spat. He returned his attention to the pump and made sure that it was working properly. 'We don't need much,' he called to Clancy. Then he stood up and walked to the cliff edge. He peered down into the misty cloud.

'They're pretty powerful. Like I said, one egg pod can power a spaceship. But these have been lying around for ages. We'll have to see what we can get out of them. Before that, we need to get back down.'

Fleming stood back from the edge and then turned round to look at Rory. 'And now we've finished using the winch to bring stuff up, we can use it to send things down.'

'I can climb,' Rory protested. He didn't want to be winched several thousand feet. 'If I'm going down, that is.'

'What are you talking about?' Fleming asked.

'You said I wasn't going back,' Rory replied.

Fleming pulled Rory to his feet and ran the end of the cable that was connected to the winch through his prisoner's climbing harness. He then yanked Rory to the edge of the crater.

'Unfortunately, I need you,' Fleming said. 'You're the only one who can make Angela better. So you've got to go back down.'

Rory peered over the side. It certainly was a very long way down. Perhaps it was better to travel by winch, after all. He looked back and saw that although the cable was attached to the winch, there was a loose pile of it that hadn't been fed back on the machine.

'Hang on,' Rory said. 'You need to…'

'We need to get down in a hurry,' Fleming whispered in his ear. 'You'd better hope the cable is strong enough to take the strain.'

Rory opened his mouth to argue, but Fleming put a large hand in the middle of his back and pushed. Rory found himself falling through the air with the cable streaming out above him. Rory screamed as he fell.

Makron helped guide the Doctor and Amy through the secret tunnel and out into the open sea beyond Reef. While Amy enjoyed the new sights and the different beings she met while travelling with the Doctor, she was glad they were heading back to *The Ocean Explorer.*

'What do you think's been happening on the sub?' Amy asked.

'I'm not sure,' the Doctor said. He was concentrating on the sub's controls.

'Rory's probably been having a whale of a time!' she joked.

The Doctor looked up. 'What?' he asked. 'Oh yes. "Whale". Very good, Pond!"'

Then one of the instruments on the control panel began to buzz.

'It's a signal,' the Doctor said. 'It's very weak but it might be the submarine!'

He set the engines to go as fast as they could. As they sped along, the Doctor asked Makron about his people.

'Tell me, Makron, how do your people work with electricity under water? Usually the two don't mix very well!'

The translator flashed and the computer voice said: 'You humans have blood running through your veins. The Shoal have blood, but we also have electricity in our bodies. Almost all the sea creatures on Hydron do.'

'So it's like a natural thing?' Amy asked.

'Yes. We can feed on it and use it before we even hatch from our eggs.'

'So the Shoal lay eggs,' the Doctor said. 'Of course you do. Sorry.'

'Like a chicken!' Amy said.

The Doctor shushed her. 'Chicken's eggs have a yolk which is full of food for the baby chick to feed on. The Shoal eggs don't have a yolk. Instead they have some form of electrical charge stored in the roe somehow.'

'We need very large amounts of energy to survive while we are in our eggs.'

'And that's how the low swimmers can electrocute people with their lures?'

'That's right,' Makron said. 'The low swimmers can focus the electricity in their lures and use it as a weapon, but the high and medium swimmers can only use it to power torches or other items that need electricity when we touch them.'

'Once a year, all members of the Shoal who want to have children swim to the spawning grounds,' Makron explained through the Doctor's translator. 'There are many Founts on Hydron, but different ones are used each year depending on the moons and the tides.'

While they were talking, *The Verne* was homing in on the signal the Doctor had picked up when they left Reef. A red warning light began to flash on the control panel telling them they were getting closer to whatever was sending the signal.

While the Doctor attended to the controls, Amy thought she had better continue the conversation to find out all they could about the Shoal.

'What's a Fount?' she asked.

'A Fount is an amazing sea mountain,' Makron told her. 'It rises into the air as high as the sea is deep. At the top are pools of the purest water.'

The Doctor's hands flowed across the controls as if he had been driving submersibles his whole life. Then he turned back to Makron. 'Your whole culture is based on electricity, even though you live underwater!' the Doctor said. 'And how quickly do the Shoal grow once the eggs have been laid?'

'We hatch in a matter of days,' Makron said. 'We are almost fully grown then. We can swim and eat normally. We don't need the electricity to feed on any more. But we have changed from needing fresh water to live in to needing salt water.'

'Aha!' the Doctor said. 'Just like salmon on Earth. They swim up river from the sea and lay their eggs.' He chuckled. 'This mad old universe!'

'We have to leave the Founts as soon as we can, otherwise we'd die. We have to go down the Drops!'

Before Amy could ask what the Drops were, the

buzzing on the control panel became a bleeping. The Doctor had brought the submersible to the surface of the sea and gentle waves lapped at the view screen in front of the pilots' seats. Twenty metres away was a small, grey object that was smaller than *The Verne*.

'What's that?' Amy asked. It certainly wasn't *The Ocean Explorer*.

'I would say it is an emergency buoy of some kind,' the Doctor said. 'They probably launched it when we went missing. I wonder why they didn't wait for us?'

Makron flashed turquoise and green. 'They were attacked by the low swimmers,' the machine translated.

'What?' Amy looked shocked.

'My father gave Admiral Icktheus permission to give the crew aboard *The Ocean Explorer* a virus,' Makron explained.

The Doctor did not look pleased. 'Why did he do that?' he asked.

'Because the last time there was a submarine here, they attacked us. They stole our children!' Makron flashed an angry red.

'Tell me what happened,' the Doctor said. 'I want to know everything.'

CHAPTER 14
MAKRON'S STORY

The Doctor and Amy sat and listened as Makron told them what had happened when the humans had come to his planet before.

'About a year ago there were visitors to my planet,' Makron said. 'We weren't stupid enough to think that we were the only living things in the galaxy, but it was a bit of a shock. Everything about the aliens surprised us.'

'First contact with another species is always difficult,' the Doctor said. Amy nodded. Look at what happened between the humans and Silurians on her world!

'They looked different to us and they had big

machines that they used for travelling under water.

At first we called them the "Hurry"! That's because they all wore orange when they were outside their submarine. We thought that these creatures had orange skin! We had no idea that they needed clothes to swim under the water and that, in fact, each one was a slightly different colour of white or pink or brown.'

'Hurry is a good word for humans,' the Doctor said. 'Always rushing into things.'

'The most surprising thing about them was that they didn't even notice us. Our scientists had seen their ship above our planet and then they dropped an underwater travel machine into the sea.'

'A submarine,' Amy clarified.

'Is that what they call it?' asked Makron. 'Well, we learned about this "submarine" and we were very curious. We wanted to know who they were and what they wanted. But we were scared. We wanted to have a look first, to see what these new people might be like.'

'So you followed the submarine?' the

Doctor asked.

Makron nodded. 'Yes. They were exploring and we were worried. At that time of year it was spawning season. A lot of the Shoal were making their way to the Founts. The movement of so many large creatures couldn't be hidden, though. The humans noticed and followed the Shoalys.

'I bet Admiral Icktheus was very cross!' Amy said. 'He seems the type!'

'My father wanted us to go to the humans and tell them that the Founts were sacred. Only the grown-up Shoalys can go there and they only get to go once in their lifetimes. It's a really special time of year. We have feasts and there are fun things to do.'

'Sort of like Christmas,' Amy said. She was shocked by Makron's story. She thought this sort of thing just didn't happen anymore.

'Exactly,' the Doctor replied. 'Then what happened?'

'Icktheus convinced the Assembly that they should attack the humans to show them that they were doing something wrong. There was a battle between the low swimmers and the humans.'

Makron paused. His mouth opened and closed several times as if he was uncomfortable.

The Doctor bowed his head. 'I am sorry if this is difficult,' he said.

Makron's eyes closed. 'The humans did something terrible,' he said. 'I don't know how they did it but they poisoned the water of the Fount. The whole Assembly wanted the humans dead then. So the low swimmers attacked the submarine.'

'And it sank,' the Doctor said. 'Was everyone aboard killed?'

'There weren't any onboard,' Makron said. They had all gone to the Fount,' Makron replied.

'I was right!' the Doctor sighed. 'The humans were hiding something. I don't know if Captain Clancy is involved but Mister Fleming definitely knows about this previous mission.'

'Not long after the spaceship took the surviving humans away and we never saw them again – until now.'

CHAPTER 15
THE WRECK

The Doctor sat back in the pilot's chair, shaking his head. Amy wiped a tear from her cheek. Makron looked sad.

'Both sides are at fault,' the Doctor said. 'However, the humans' lack of respect for your planet and people is worse than your desire to defend yourselves.'

He turned back to the controls and started getting the submersible ready to dive.

'Where are we going?' Amy asked.

'We need to stop this becoming a full scale war,' the Doctor said. 'The Shoal – or at least Admiral Icktheus and his low swimmers – are following

The Ocean Explorer. If they manage to catch up with the submarine before we do, they will sink it and kill everyone onboard.'

He set the final controls and pushed the square steering wheel forward, angling the submersible down. There was a grim expression on his face. Amy recognised it as determination.

'But what can we do in this little thing?' Amy made a circle in the air with her finger to indicate *The Verne*'s tiny interior.

'Don't worry about that,' the Doctor replied. His mouth was showing a hint of smile now. 'I have a plan…'

The refuelling was complete and *The Ocean Explorer* was already miles away from the polluted Fount. Rory was back in the medical bay looking after the sick, although now he had one of Mister Fleming's armed security guards standing over him all the time.

He had hated being pushed from the cliff top.

The fall must have taken only a few seconds but it seemed to Rory that it had taken forever. Just when he thought he was going to faint from fear, the cable snapped tight and he bounced up again. He supposed it was a bit like making an unplanned bungee jump.

It had only taken half an hour for the winch to lower him the few thousand feet to the submarine below. All that time Rory had been thinking. He was wondering how the Doctor and Amy were doing and where they could be. He hoped he would see them again soon. He missed Amy but he knew she was safe with the Doctor.

He also thought about Mister Fleming and why he wanted to take the fish creatures' egg cases. He knew it was for money, but he was shocked that some people would do anything to be rich. Rory would always rather have a clear conscience than have a lot of money. He couldn't live with himself if he did something as bad as Fleming had.

Before he and Captain Clancy had returned

to the sub, Fleming had threatened to kill them both – and the rest of the crew if Clancy didn't do exactly what Fleming wanted.

Fleming forced Rory down the ladder to the control room where two more of the security guards stood with their guns held at the ready.

'This man is under arrest,' Fleming said. 'Take him to the medical bay and watch him. If he does anything suspicious shoot him.'

Rory was pushed down the submarine's corridors at gunpoint and eventually reached the medical bay. Here, the guard stood outside the door with his gun held tightly across his chest.

'Welcome back,' said MARVE.

'Hello, MARVE,' Rory replied. 'Did you miss me?'

'No.' The robot's two camera eyes looked at Rory without emotion. Then the screen under the eyes showed a smile. 'Just kidding!'

'Ha, ha,' said Rory. 'So, what's new?'

'There has been a mutiny and Mister Fleming's

guards have taken over the submarine.'

Rory looked at the robot. 'Yeah,' he said. 'Thanks for that,' and he sank down into one of the plastic chairs by the table.

At the front of *The Ocean Explorer*, Jane Clancy was sitting in a chair that belonged to one of the control room's crew. Fleming was sitting in her command chair and she didn't like that.

The moment the submarine had dived underwater again, Fleming had ordered that one of the eggs be brought to the control room. Now it sat next to him, bobbing in its glass tube. It seemed to be pressing itself against the side of its container like a child staring through a toy shop window.

'Why is it doing that?' asked Clancy.

Fleming looked over at her. 'The eggs like being in a group, so it always points towards the largest number.'

'You're using it as a tracker?'

'You saw the lake. It was stagnant, dead. They must be using a new water volcano and this thing will tell me how to find it.'

Clancy sighed. 'That's why you needed the eggs *on-board.*'

She shook her head. She was powerless. There was nothing she could do to stop this madman. But at least she could try to find out the whole story.

'Why wasn't I told about the other submarine?' she asked. 'Why did the ompany hide this from me and my crew?'

'Because I told them to,' he said.

'Why would they do what *you* told them?' Clancy frowned. Fleming stood up and came over to the former captain. He bent down and whispered in her ear. Jane shuddered.

'I was the only one who came back from Hydron,' he said. 'I could tell them anything I liked. Who else could they ask to check that what I said was the truth?'

Clancy's eyes widened. 'You lied to them?' she breathed.

'I told them that the whole expedition had been a disaster. I told them that there were people left behind on the other submarine.'

'What?' Clancy was confused.

'I wasn't going to let the Company know about the fish eggs,' Fleming said. 'Not when I could come and take them for myself. So I told them that the fish creatures had attacked the submarine and we'd been forced to leave them and return to Earth.'

Clancy blinked at the madman. 'I get it,' she said. 'There's no way the Company would tell anyone that that had happened! The government would have closed them down.'

'You got it,' Fleming said. 'So I suggested they mount another mission with a cover story. I told them we could say there were useful mineral deposits here. I told them that when we got here I would reveal the real secret mission – to rescue the survivors.'

'Very clever,' Clancy said. 'All so you can get

your hands on the eggs.' She shook her head, disgusted. 'And how do you plan to get away with it?' she asked.

He smiled and walked back to the command chair and patted the glass tube with the pod inside.

'These egg cases are going to make me rich,' he said. 'All I need to do is find them. And when I do, I'm going to take the whole lot with me.'

'But what about the baby fish inside?'

'I'm not going to wait for them to hatch!' laughed Fleming. 'In case you've forgotten, we've got a whole ocean of fish creatures after us. We won't have time to stop.'

'But the baby fish…' gasped Clancy. 'They'll be killed.'

'So what?' Fleming said. His eyes became misty as if he was imaging himself rolling in money. 'Last time we only managed to get five. This time we'll get the whole lake full! Thousands of them. Thousands!'

The small yellow submersible moved slowly through the dark waters at the base of the undersea cliffs. The various lights on its hull shone into the gloom, picking out the volcanic rocks and nervous creatures that lived there.

Inside the cockpit, a steady beeping told the three people inside that the sub was dangerously close to the floor of the ocean and in danger of crashing into it. The Doctor ignored the sound and concentrated on the controls.

He was gently steering *The Verne* towards something that the sonar showed up as a large bump on the seabed. A readout on the control panel displayed how close they were to the "contact".

Amy looked at the green, digital display. It read 8.73 metres. Everyone was holding their breath. Even the Doctor was biting his lip.

Makron leaned forward and flashed a question. 'Will we be able to get onboard?'

The Doctor didn't answer at first. He was still concentrating. The green numbers flicked down and down. 5.68, 5.03...

'If it looks okay...' The Doctor moved the position of the outside light. Suddenly a great big grey figure filled the screens. 'There she is!' he laughed and clapped his hands.

Amy couldn't help smiling, too.

The Verne moved forward, over the sunken wreck of a submarine. It was *The Marine Adventurer*, the one that the Shoal had sunk when the humans had last visited Hydron.

'She's still airtight,' the Doctor said, reading a computer screen.

'What does that mean?' asked Amy.

'It means that the submarine still might be working!'

CHAPTER 16
THE DOCTOR TO THE RESCUE!

Rory was hunched over a microscope, peering down at the image of the virus. With nothing he could do to escape, Rory had decided to double check MARVE's test results to see if there really was no cure for the virus. As far as he could see the robot had been right. They could give the patients medicines and antibiotics, but all this did was bring down their temperatures.

Suddenly, he felt the deck of the submarine tilt. He looked down at his feet. They were surfacing! He stood up, turned and went to the door. The security guard was standing opposite him in the corridor. He looked at Rory without expression.

'What's happening?' Rory asked.

'We must have reached the next water volcano,' the guard said. 'Captain Fleming is bringing the sub up so that we can radio the drop ship.'

'Why can't you just radio underwater?'

'You can't use a radio underwater. It's like being underground. The signal can't get through. You need to have an aerial on the surface.'

Rory looked at him and then his eyebrows lowered. 'Hang on. Drop ship? You mean *The Cosmic Rover?*'

The guard nodded.

As *The Ocean Explorer's* periscope broke the surface of the purple sea, it left a v-shape of bubbles behind it. Then, bit by bit, the tower emerged from the water, before finally, the rest of the deck emerged, ploughing through the waves. The hatch on top of the tower opened and Fleming climbed out onto the slippery metal.

He looked out over the rail at the mountain

that lay ahead of the sub. It was different from the last one. The rock was a different colour – more brown than grey. He brought a pair of binoculars to his eyes for a better look and saw that there was even a more level piece of land at the edge of the sea.

It didn't matter. His plan didn't involve climbing up the cliffs. Not this time. Instead, he would radio the spaceship in orbit above them. The automatic pilot would bring the ship down into the atmosphere of Hydron and collect *The Ocean Explorer* in its huge metal clamps. Then it could lift the sub over the top of the mountain and drop it in the freshwater lake at the summit. This might kill a few of the fish creatures, but that didn't matter to him.

He was going to kill them all anyway with *The Cosmic Rover*'s lasers. Then he could collect all the eggs and leave this stupid, purple planet forever. He'd sell the eggs to the Company and retire to Catrigan Nova with its whirlpools of gold. Easy.

Without warning, a hundred low swimmers appeared in the water about a kilometre to the right, off the starboard bow. With them, they seemed to have a dozen or so larger fish. Fleming lowered the binoculars. Whatever they had, he didn't care. This time, he was ready for them. This time, it would be them sinking to the bottom of the sea.

'Have you signalled the drop ship?' he asked, speaking into his radio.

'Yes, Sir,' a voice crackled back.

'Good. Then arm the torpedoes!' He jumped down through the hatch and closed the doorway above him. 'And prepare the poison!' he shouted.

He slid down the ladder and came to a halt in the control room.

'We have 124 contacts, Mister Fleming,' one of the crew reported. 'They're maintaining a distance of 800 metres.'

'Staying put, eh?' Fleming laughed. 'Then they'll be sitting targets.'

He sat down in the command chair and

listened as the crew reported the situation, and the submarine dipped beneath the water once more.

'Contacts now 300 metres.'

'Fire the forward torpedoes! All tubes!' bellowed Fleming.

Another of the crew in black coveralls pressed some buttons and six small lights on his panel lit up. 'Six tubes armed and ready,' the woman said.

'Wait!' Jane Clancy shouted. She had to try one last time. 'Please don't do this. You'll be starting a war with those creatures.'

Fleming looked at her. His face was red with anger. 'How dare you challenge me?' he screamed. He jumped up from his chair and grabbed the nearest armed guard. He dragged the unfortunate crewman over to where Jane was sitting. 'I am relieving Captain Clancy of her command. If she does that again – shoot her!'

He marched forward and stood right in front of the screens and next to the female guard. With a brief look of defiance at Clancy, Fleming pressed each of the lights on the torpedo control panel in turn.

'Fire!' he hissed.

WHOOOSH!

The torpedoes left the nose of the submarine and disappeared into the darkness, leaving a cloud of bubbles.

Ping.

The sonar sounded as the sound waves reflected from the underwater missiles.

Ping-ping-ping.

The pings became faster as the torpedoes got closer to their targets. Fleming clenched his fist. He knew the first weapon would strike home any second.

Ping-ping-ping-pi...

The sonar went silent.

'What's going on?' Fleming looked down at the woman sitting at the torpedo control panel.

'The torpedoes have been...' she shrugged, 'They've been switched off, Sir.'

'Switched off?' Fleming was about to start

shouting again, but then something hit the submarine. The impact threw Fleming forward and he hit his head on the corner of the screen. He sat down on the floor and put his hand to his head. When he took it away his fingers had blood on them.

'Get that nurse boy up here,' he said, looking at his hand. Then he looked up as if he was seeing the control room for the first time. A guard jumped forward and helped Fleming to his feet. 'What hit us?' Fleming asked.

The sonar operator hesitated.

'Well?' demanded Fleming.

'The computer says it was another submarine, Sir.'

'Impossible! The fish creatures must have a device that reflects sonar images or something.' Fleming smiled. A trickle of blood came down his forehead and caught in his eyebrow. 'It doesn't matter what they have. Is the poison ready?'

'Yes, Sir. The tanks have been filled with

7D-24.'

'But that will kill everything closer than 100 metres to the ship almost instantly!' Clancy said.

Rory arrived in the control room with his guard. He looked at Fleming and his bleeding head.

'Exactly!' Fleming looked at Jane with a shark-like grin. Then he placed a hand on the shoulder of his crewman operating the water tanks. 'Release the poison!'

CREEEEEEEEEEEEEEEEEEK...

An ear-piercing noise filled the submarine and made Rory's teeth feel strange. It was a really loud, high-pitched buzzing as if there were a million angry bees behind the sub's walls.

'I WOULDN'T DO THAT IF I WERE YOU!'

Everyone looked about. The voice had come from all around them.

'Who is that?' shouted Fleming.

Rory smiled, walked forward and spoke to the room as if he was talking to an invisible magic creature.

'Hello, Doctor!' he said.

'HELLO, RORY!' the voice boomed back. Rory smiled the biggest smile.

'Hello, Amy!' Rory called.

'The Doctor? But he's dead,' Fleming said.

'LIKE MOST OF MY ENEMIES, YOU'VE DISCOVERED I'M A BIT DIFFICULT TO KILL!' There was a sort of muffled sound of the Doctor talking to someone else.

The screen at the front of the control room flickered and then filled with the Doctor's face.

'Is that better?' he asked. 'Not so loud?'

'I am the captain of this submarine,' Fleming screamed at the Doctor's face.

'No, you're not,' the Doctor replied. 'Jane Clancy is.'

Jane lifted her chin and smiled.

'You have no authority here, Doctor!' Fleming yelled.

'Oh, stop shouting,' the Doctor said. 'I have every right to replace you with a frog if I want to, and don't think I'm not tempted. But Captain Jane is a good woman and, right now, I need her.'

'I thought we were under attack,' Rory said.

'Ah well, I hooked up the sonic screwdriver to this submarine's sonar system and deployed what they call a "towed array" – that's a whole load of microphones basically. But I turned them into speakers. Anyway, when I switched it to maximum, it knocked out all the low swimmers.'

'But *The Verne* doesn't have a towed array,' said Jane, standing up.

'That's because I'm not on *The Verne*!' The Doctor's smile filled the screen. 'I'm on *The Marine Adventurer*!' For a moment the picture changed to that of the large, grey submarine – the mirror image of its sister ship, *The Ocean Explorer*.

'That's impossible,' breathed Fleming.

Rory looked at him. 'Yeah,' he said. 'The Doctor's like that!'

'But we don't have very much time before the low swimmers wake up with nasty headaches and probably in very bad moods!' The Doctor peered at them all and then he smiled again. 'But I'm sure we can sort everything out.'

'What do you need us to do?' asked Jane.

'Lock him up for a start,' the Doctor stabbed a finger at the screen. He was pointing at Fleming.

'With pleasure,' said Captain Jane. She marched up to Fleming and then turned to a pair of guards. 'If you know what's good for you, you will do what I say and put this man in the brig. He is no longer an officer on this ship nor is he head of security.'

The two security guards looked at one another and then jumped forward. They each grabbed an arm and took Fleming away.

'Right,' the Doctor said. 'Don't forget that Doctor Angela Morton will need arresting as soon as she recovers. Now! I'd like some of the crew of *The Ocean Explorer* to go with Makron here. He needs to rescue his father and the rest of the Shoal from Admiral Icktheus.' He paused. 'You won't know what I'm talking about, but let's join the submarines and have a quick chat.'

'How do we join up the subs?' Rory asked.

'I don't know, Rory,' the Doctor said. 'Have you got any boat ties?' His smile became even wider than normal. 'Boat ties are cool!'

CHAPTER 17
THE FINAL MISSION

Half an hour later, they were all standing in the control room, preparing for their final mission. Once the submarines had surfaced, the crew had attached them together using ropes that they were now calling "boat ties". The Doctor and Amy had come aboard and some crewmembers were already with Makron and had swapped over to *The Marine Adventurer*, which was preparing to go on its rescue mission to Reef.

The Doctor sat with Amy, opposite Rory and Captain Jane. He was explaining what they were about to do. 'We need to get up to the freshwater lake on top of the Fount – the water volcano. We need to return the eggs aboard this submarine to their rightful place.'

'Fleming has sent a message to our spaceship,' Jane explained. 'He was going to use it to pick up the sub and drop it at the top of the mountain. It'll be here in about ninety minutes.'

'That's good,' the Doctor replied. 'We'll need to be leaving soon anyway. But we can't be dropped in the lake; that would kill any Shoalys in the way.'

The Doctor operated a control and the viewscreen flicked to show a diagram of the water volcano. Rory could see on it that the mountain was hollow. It was a bit like a basin made of stone with the lake of water at the top. The sides of the mountain came down below the level of the sea and then flattened to become the seabed.

'What's that?' Rory asked, bending forward. He pointed at a line that ran from the ocean floor right up to the bottom of the pool.

'I'm glad you asked that,' the Doctor said. 'Because that is where we need to take this submarine up to, so we can get the eggs back to their nursery.'

'We have to take *The Verne* up there? It looks very small,' said Captain Clancy.

Amy shook her head. 'We can't fit all the eggs in there.' She frowned. 'We have to go in this one.'

'You want to pilot *The Ocean Explorer* up through those narrow caves?' Jane shook her head. 'We can't do that. We'll never fit.'

'We have to try,' the Doctor said. 'Don't worry, I'll be here to help.' Then he leaned forward. 'One more thing.'

'Yes?'

'By the time we get going, the low swimmers will be waking up, so they'll probably be following us, trying to stop us.'

'We'd better get started, then,' Captain Jane said.

The Doctor jumped forward and kissed her cheek. 'Thank you,' he said.

Jane blushed and then clicked on the viewscreen.

An image of Makron appeared. He was standing next to a crewman with a blue uniform. 'How are we doing with *The Marine Adventurer*?' she asked.

'Casting off now, ma'am,' the crewman said.

'Keep hold of that translator, Makron!' the Doctor said.

'I will,' the Shoaly replied.

'And don't forget our plan!'

'No, Doctor, I won't. As soon as I have freed my dad, I'll send help!'

'We might well need it. I have a feeling that Admiral Icktheus won't be in a forgiving mood.'

Amy heard a couple of clunks as the two submarines separated once more.

'Good luck!' Makron said, glowing turquoise and yellow.

'And to you!' Amy called.

The screen went blank and the Doctor sat down in one of the sub's pilot seats.

Because there were more crew aboard the other submarine now, the Doctor, Amy and Rory would all have to help steer and control *The Ocean Explorer*. Rory sat in the one of the pilot's seats while the Doctor and Amy went over to sit at the master control panel.

'All ready?' Captain Jane asked.

Rory started to say 'Geronim...'

'Don't say it!' The Doctor looked at him sternly. Then he turned round and muttered, 'That's my line.'

Rory nodded. 'Oh. Okay,' he said. 'Um, "yes", then!'

The captain issued her orders and the Doctor and Rory started to steer the submarine down through the sea. Amy counted off the depth every time they passed a depth ten metres more than the last.

As they passed 400 metres, the aft sonar began to ping quietly. 'Looks like we've got company,' Amy said.

'The low swimmers are awake and they probably know where we are,' the Doctor said. 'It won't take long for them to figure out what we're doing.'

'Where's this tunnel entrance?' asked Rory.

'It's deep,' the Doctor said. 'About 630 metres.'

'Don't submarines collapse if they go too far down?' asked Amy.

'*The Ocean Explorer* has a crush depth of about 650 metres,' Captain Jane said. 'We should be okay.'

For the next few minutes they dived in silence, with only the quiet ping of the sonar reminding them that they were not alone in the murky depths.

Finally, the depth gauge read 627 metres when the Doctor pointed to something on the screen. The forward lights played on the seabed and illuminated a jagged black hole ahead and below.

'Are we really going to fit through that?' asked Jane. 'We'd better slow down so we can steer more easily.'

The Doctor and Rory pulled back on their wheels and the submarine slowed, nosing forward, bit by bit, into the underwater tunnel.

'Breathe in!' the Doctor joked. Amy smiled, but

the other two looked very serious. She coughed and went back to checking the sonar.

'Amy, I need you to monitor the forward sonar now,' Captain Jane said.

'We'll just have to assume we're being followed,' the Doctor added.

Amy nodded and switched the sonar controls so that the alert would sound if the submarine was too close to the edge of the cave. The sonar would also be able to map what the tunnel looked like.

'Ah,' said Rory. 'We might have a problem.'

On the screen, the sonar was showing an image of the tunnel, sideways on. They could all see that instead of sloping up, the tunnel seemed to be heading down. The depth gauge read 638 metres now.

As it passed the crush depth of 650 metres, the submarine began to creak. Amy looked about nervously.

'Don't worry,' said Jane. 'When they build these things they always allow for a bit either way with the collapse depth.' She didn't sound convinced.

'She'll hold together,' the Doctor said.

There was another menacing creak and a tiny spurt of water sprayed in Rory's face. He flapped his arms about. The Doctor dug in his pocket and pulled out a piece of modelling clay. He reached across and placed it over the small hole.

The depth reading flicked to 656 meters.

'Do you know what sardines call a submarine?'

'Oh no,' Amy said. 'Not another one of your jokes.'

'A can of people!'

Rory moaned.

'I just thought that if we can't raise the submarine, we might raise a smile,' the Doctor explained.

At that moment, the numbers on the depth gauge changed to 655.

'We're going back up!' Rory said. The screen showed that the tunnel was indeed rising now.

'Okay,' the Doctor nodded. 'I suggest we get a

move on.'

'Very well,' Clancy said. 'Increase speed. But, please, don't break my submarine.'

On the screen, the sonar image showed that the tunnel sloped upwards, becoming steeper and steeper until it was almost like a lift shaft, pointing up vertically. Jane ordered that they increase speed and it felt more like they were in a spaceship or aeroplane taking off, rather than in a submarine.

As they climbed through the underground tunnels, the water flowing in the other direction became faster and faster. This meant that they had to increase the speed of the submarine, but it also meant that they didn't have very much time to react to how the tunnel changed course.

The Ocean Explorer was jolting left and right and Rory was thrown this way and that in his seat as the submarine sped up the tunnel.

Every now and then the big metal bulk of the sub would emerge from one part of the tunnel into a new section that had air in it as well.

Amy looked at the water as it pounded on the viewscreen and realised that this is exactly what the Shoal had to do to reach their spawning ground. She was amazed by Makron's people and she hoped they made it out alive and as good friends.

There was a sickening crash as the submarine broke through the pouring water once more and smashed into the wall of rock beside it. A jagged piece of the cliff ripped through the front of the submarine, missing the Doctor and Rory by less than a metre. Water poured in through the gash, and the viewscreens exploded.

Then the engines faltered. The power flickered on and off. If they didn't make it now, they would fall back down the waterfall and into the sea far below. With the hole in the submarine, the control room would fill with water in a moment and they would all drown.

The Doctor threw his hand down hard on the button that controlled the power levels in the engines. They were trying to switch themselves off, but he wasn't having it.

'Noooooooooo,' he shouted, his face screwed up with effort.

As he kept the button pressed down with one hand, his other was pushing the square control wheel as far forward as he could – keeping the submarine at maximum speed.

Then, with a final burst of power, *The Ocean Explorer* jumped forward. Rory glimpsed the purple sky of Hydron through the gaping hole in the sub's nose. There were in mid air!

'GERONIMO!' the Doctor called as the sub began to fall back to the water.

The Ocean Explorer crashed into the side of the crater and swayed from side to side before coming to stop at a strange angle, like a beached whale.

'So… it's okay for you to say it…' Rory began to complain.

'Eggs!' the Doctor shouted and ran off through the control room, heading for the secret lab. They all raced after him. When they got there, the Doctor grabbed two of the glass tubes and the other three took one each.

They staggered through the twisted corridors of the submarine up to the hatch in the side of the tower.

'I'm sorry,' the Doctor said to Captain Clancy.

'What for?' she breathed. 'We made it!'

'I know,' the Doctor unlocked the metal door. 'But I did break your submarine.' He kicked open the hatch and stepped out into the sunlight.

A hundred low swimmers had surrounded the crashed ship and had their forked weapons all pointed at the Doctor.

Admiral Icktheus stepped forward and his skin pulsed angrily.

'Kill the humans!'

CHAPTER 18
ARRIVALS AND DEPARTURES

I don't think you want to do that, Admiral,' the Doctor replied.

Icktheus stared in horror at what the Doctor was holding. He recognised the small, dark balls in the glass tubes instantly.

'Lower your weapons!' he ordered his commandos. *'He has the roe!'*

The soldiers did as they were told.

Rory stepped out beside the Doctor and Amy followed him, with Jane bringing up the rear.

'Now what?' Amy asked. 'We can't hold these eggs hostage.'

'We're not holding them hostage,' the Doctor said. 'We're just holding them! I'd never do anything to hurt them. Now, Admiral Icktheus, on the other hand, has a nasty little mind so he thinks nasty little thoughts. Without asking us, he has assumed we are doing what he would do.'

'That doesn't answer the question, Doctor,' Amy looked sideways at him.

'We just have to wait.'

'What?'

'For Makron and his father!'

Almost as he spoke, there was a deep, loud flapping sound. A vast flying fish the size of an airliner appeared above the edge of the crater and then landed in the lake. On its back, there were thirty or so Shoal members. Amy recognised Makron and Darkin among them.

Darkin climbed down from the flying fish and approached Icktheus. Makron ran along behind, holding the Doctor's translation device.

'Stop this, Icktheus,' Darkin said. 'These creatures are not our enemies.'

'You are soft and weak,' Icktheus replied. 'I have over one hundred troops. You have a handful. I will not surrender my advantage that easily, Governor!'

'I thought you would say that,' Darkin said. At that moment, an even louder flapping sound filled the air. It was coming from everywhere. More than fifty flying fish appeared, surrounding the top of the water volcano. Each had thirty or so low swimmers on their backs, all wearing the belt of purple seaweed that represented the Assembly.

Icktheus bowed his head. He knew he had lost. Two of the Assembly's low swimmers stepped forward and locked the admiral's fins in what looked like silver handcuffs.

'You are under arrest for treason, Admiral,' Darkin said. 'I will see to it that you will have a fair trial.'

The admiral was led away onto the back of one

of the flying fish. With an enormous roar from its huge wings, it lifted into the air and dived down, away from the Fount.

The Doctor handed one of his jars to Rory and then climbed down the submarine's external ladder. He rushed forward to greet Darkin and Makron.

'These are yours, I think,' he said showing the high swimmers the tube with the eggs in it.

'They can join the others,' Darkin said.

The Doctor looked at the beautiful, violet coloured water of the lake. It was full of the dark fish eggs. He smiled. 'May we?' he asked.

'By all means.'

The Doctor waved his companions and Captain Clancy over to him. They climbed down the ladder, careful not to disturb the eggs in their protective tubes. Amy reached the Doctor first.

'Go on, then,' the Doctor said, gesturing at the water.

Amy didn't have to be told twice. She unscrewed

the lid of the tube and bent down by the water's edge. Then she gently poured the liquid into the lake. With a satisfying splash, the egg tumbled into the Fount. Rory and Jane did the same as the Doctor added the last two.

'All safe and sound,' he said.

'Not bad for a day's work,' Rory agreed.

'We stopped a war,' Amy added.

'And returned some baby fish to their nursery,' Clancy reminded them.

'Not a nursery,' the Doctor said, looking stern.

'What?'

'Baby fish don't go to nursery,' he said.

'No?' Jane was confused.

'Baby fish go to plaice school.'

Both Amy and Rory started hitting the Doctor's arm.

'Ow! Stop that!' he said, laughing.

'Only if you stop telling such rubbish jokes,' said Amy.

'I promise,' the Doctor said. 'Cross my hearts.'

Suddenly, there was another loud whooshing sound. It wasn't the flying fish this time, but something much bigger: *The Cosmic Rover*. It glided down through the clouds and sat above the mountain awaiting instructions like an enormous, obedient dog. Captain Jane took out her radio and started talking to the onboard computer.

'Ah,' the Doctor said. 'The ship. Excellent. Yes, I think we should get back, find the TARDIS and then...'

'The Tower of London?' Amy asked.

'Ha! Yes. The Tower of London.'

Captain Jane finished talking to the ship on her radio and stepped forward. She put her head on one side, looking at the Doctor as if he was a complicated painting she was trying to work out. 'You're not really from Head Office are you?' she asked. 'You're not really in charge of Health and Safety?'

The Doctor put his hands on hers and bowed his head to her ear. 'That depends,' he said quietly.

'What on?' she whispered back.

'Whose health and safety you're talking about!'

THE END

DOCTOR WHO

RAIN OF TERROR

MIKE TUCKER

CHAPTER 1
DEATH FROM THE SKY

It was the best holiday that Gellen had ever had. Her father and Amanda – his girlfriend – had been hinting about some kind of surprise for her birthday for weeks, but hadn't given any hint as to what it might be. Gellen had been sure that it was either going to be a trip to the alien zoo on the far side of the Moon or, at best, to the National Museum of Mars, but when the bus had pulled up outside their little flat in Brighton with the words 'Galactic Safari' in big bright letters on the side, Gellen had known that they were going much,

much further.

At first she had been excited, but as the video they showed on the bus explained how long the trip was going to take, Gellen started to get a bit scared.

Her father had hugged her and told her that there was nothing to be worried about. He used the hyper-sleep chambers on the deep space shuttles all the time. After that Gellen started to feel better. Her dad was an engineer for one of the big colony builders, and was always spending weeks – sometimes months – on faraway planets with exotic sounding names. It was why he and mum had split up.

Gellen wished that her mum could have come on the trip too, but she was grown-up enough to realise that a holiday with all three of them wasn't going to happen again. Before she had left, her mum had turned up at the house with a present; a holo-recorder so that Gellen could record everything that she was going to see. Gellen was determined that she would make a full record to show her mum when she got back to Earth.

That had only been a week ago, but as far as Gellen was concerned it felt like a lifetime. Her dad had been right about the hyper-sleep. She had gone to sleep in a strange plastic cocoon before the shuttle even left the ground and the next thing she knew she had been waking up in orbit around Xirrinda.

Since then they had taken antigravity balloon trips over the canopy forest of Brinti, swum in the bubbling lake at Ortagon (which had been like swimming in a fizzy drink) and eaten more fancy food than Gellen had ever realised existed.

To end their trip, they were spending a couple of days at a treetop hotel on the edge of the grassy plains of the Xirrinda Wildlife Preserve, and Gellen had been spending all of her time capturing holo-recordings of the local animals. She had been amazed by the vast variety of creatures that roamed through the long, waving grass. Huge herds of the six-legged, horse-like things that the locals called Trinto were the most common. However, there were also Beslons (house-sized insects that occasionally lumbered across the horizon) and flocks of brightly coloured birds with hollow tail feathers that made whistling sounds as they flew. Plus, according to the guide book, there was a long, thin creature called the Sharkwolf, a fearsome predator that only came out at night.

Gellen really hoped to see one of those before they went home. The picture of it in the book looked really cool. Apparently the best time to see one was dusk and so, having gone to bed on time without complaint, she now sat cross-legged on the veranda outside her bedroom, the holo-recorder set to night vision mode, the glow from the little LED screen casting a pale green light on her face.

On the screen the grassland was as clear and bright as if it was daylight. Gellen could see the long necks of a herd of Trinto bobbing up and down in the distance, and could just make out the mournful, cow-like noise that they made. She had enough pictures of Trinto. She panned the camera, studying the screen carefully, watching for the distinctive shape of the elusive Sharkwolf.

As she watched, a sudden movement made her start. She swung the camera back and pressed the zoom button. The Trinto were running, stampeding, as if something was chasing them. One of them fell, sending up a flurry of dry dirt. Another toppled into the grass, followed by another and another. Gellen's heart started to race as the distant cries grew louder and more frightened. There was another noise too, a high-pitched whistling, like a rocket on fireworks night…

Bang!

Gellen jumped as something hard landed on the wooden roof of her cabin.

Bang! Bang!

Two more impacts made her scramble to her feet. Something rolled off the roof and landed with a clatter on the veranda. From the room below she could hear her dad and Amanda. They had obviously heard the noises too. Gellen fumbled with the camera, switching it from night vision to floodlight mode. Something small and round shone in the harsh light. It looked like a small, brown pebble.

Gellen knelt down to get a better look at it. It was glossy and smooth, about the size of a large egg but slightly flattened, like the stones that her father had taught her to skim across the water at Lake Ortagon. As Gellen reached out towards the pebble it made a sharp cracking sound, and rocked backwards on the wooden slats of the veranda. Gellen snatched her hand back as the pebble shook violently to and fro. She was about to call for her father when the pebble suddenly split down each side, revealing a dark, wet interior.

Gellen watched, horrified, as dozens of thin, stick-like legs emerged from the 'pebble' and it rose up, its feet making tapping noises on the wood. Two more of the pebble creatures scuttled up onto the veranda, clustering together and making strange whispering sounds.

Gellen backed away, but as she did so her foot scuffed on the floor and the three creatures spun around. Even though they had no visible eyes it was as if they were looking at her. Slowly they started to move across the veranda towards her. Then, with horrible sucking noises, the front of all three 'pebbles' peeled back like a banana skin to reveal row after row of razor sharp teeth.

Gellen screamed.

Out in the depths of space, a police box that was

not really a police box at all hung against the stars, twirling slowly.

Inside, in the huge multi-levelled control room that should not have been able to fit inside the police box, the traveller known as the Doctor was wiping mud from the console with a large spotted handkerchief. In this incarnation – his eleventh – the Doctor was a tall, gangly young man, with a thin face and a mop of tousled hair. He was dressed in a comfortable tweed jacket and trousers. Although his face was youthful, a bow tie and colourful braces gave him the look of a much older man, though no one ever guessed that he was in fact over 900 years old.

'Please tell me we are never going there again,' groaned Amy.

The Doctor looked up as two people emerged from one of the console room's many doors. Amy and her husband, Rory, were his latest travelling companions, and they too were splattered with mud. Amy was rubbing at her flame-red hair with a large towel and glaring at him. Rory just looked miserable. The Doctor smiled apologetically.

'Yes. Well. Aridian Mire Beasts – even super-evolved Mire Beasts like those ones – are still very fond of… mire.' He folded up the handkerchief and stuck it into his jacket pocket. 'So, enough of mud, enough of Aridian revolutions, I think that we deserve… a party!'

'A party?' Amy glanced at Rory, not sure if the Doctor was joking or not.

'Yes, a party!' The Doctor started punching at controls on the console.

'Do you really think we're going to get in to any kind of party looking like this?' Rory tugged at his mud-stained shirt.

'Oh yes.' The Doctor nodded vigorously. 'You can get in anywhere if you're wearing a bow tie. Bow ties are coo…'

He didn't finish his sentence. Suddenly the

control room was filled with a deafening noise, as if a thousand tiny hammers were beating on the battered wooden shell. There was a sickening jolt as the TARDIS lurched to one side.

Peter Jenkins heard his daughter scream and raced up the stairs, terrified of what he might find. Gellen was backed against the railing on her veranda, three of the pebble creatures scuttling towards her, hissing angrily. With a cry of rage, Peter kicked out at them, sending them clattering off the edge of the veranda. Hoisting Gellen onto his shoulder he stumbled back down the stairs.

From all over the hotel he could hear the screams of holidaymakers and the hiss of the creatures. On the roof he could hear thump following thump as more of the pebbles dropped from the sky.

He kicked open the door and raced out into the car park, fumbling in his pocket for the key to the jeep he had hired. Brown pebbles littered the ground, some of them already starting to open. Sharp cracking sounds filled the night air.

With a musical beep the door to the jeep swung open and he bundled Gellen inside. She scrambled across the seat.

'Come on,' she screamed. 'Get in!'

One of the pebbles landed on the roof and Peter batted it away with the back of his hand.

'I can't.' He reached out and squeezed Gellen's hand. 'Amanda is still inside. Those things… they bit her. She can't walk. I can't leave her.'

He shut the door of the jeep and pressed another button on the key. The engine hummed into life. Gellen stared at him wide-eyed through the window.

'What are you doing?'

'The jeep is pre-programmed to take you back to the terminal. Tell your mother…' Peter smiled at his daughter. 'Tell her that I'm sorry…'

Peter stepped back as the jeep started to pull out of the car park. Gellen's terrified face was pressed against the window, screaming for him to stop. With a deep breath Peter watched his daughter vanish into the night. She was safe.

He turned back towards the hotel. The air was thick with falling pebbles, the noise of hissing creatures louder than ever. A dozen or more were advancing across the car park towards him. The creatures bared their teeth.

And surged forward.

The noise inside the TARDIS was deafening. It reminded Amy of the time she had been out in her aunt's shed during a hailstorm, listening to the tiny lumps of ice clatter on the corrugated iron roof.

Rory was hanging onto one of the handrails as the TARDIS tipped and swayed. The Doctor was wedged up against the console, his nose pressed against the scanner screen.

'What's happening?' cried Amy, hanging onto Rory.

'We've drifted into the path of an asteroid storm!' shouted the Doctor. 'But the readings... the readings are strange...'

There was a bang and a shower of sparks from the console.

'Rory! Come and hold this lever down. I want to get a sample!'

Rory staggered over to the Doctor and grabbed hold of the lever that he had indicated. The Doctor dashed across the console room, vanishing through a doorway, emerging a few moments later clutching a large fishing net.

'Amy,' he cried. 'I need you to hang on!'

'To what?'

'Me!'

The Doctor staggered towards the doors, arms and legs everywhere, like a dizzy giraffe. Amy launched herself after him.

'What are you planning to do?' she bellowed.

'A bit of fishing!' he grinned at her. 'We'll open the door, stick my net out, catch one of the meteorite thingies and have a proper look at it. Hang onto my braces would you?'

Before Amy could object, he pulled open the TARDIS doors and leaned out into space.

With a little cry of alarm Amy reached out to grab hold of him. Behind her she could hear another little cry from Rory as the two of them teetered dangerously in the TARDIS doorway.

It took all of Amy's strength to hang onto the Doctor as he lunged this way and that, before finally, with a whoop of triumph, he staggered backwards, something nestling in his net.

'Got one! Ha, hah!'

He slammed the doors shut and hurried over to the console, rummaging in the net. To Amy's surprise he pulled out a smooth, shiny pebble. Not what she was expecting at all. Weren't meteorites all pitted and jagged?

The Doctor placed it carefully on the console. Amy and Rory hurried to his side.

'Now then,' he murmured. 'Let's get a proper look at you.'

He whipped his sonic screwdriver from his jacket and flicked it into life, its lime green light washing over the strange meteorite. The Doctor peered at the read-out, puzzled.

'That's strange. That's very strange. It's generating massive gravitational interference. No wonder the console was affected.'

He picked up the pebble and as he did so it snapped open with a sharp crack. Rory and Amy jumped backwards in alarm. To Amy's horror, the inside of the pebble was lined with teeth. Rows and rows of razor sharp teeth!

'Woaah!'

The Doctor dropped the pebble as the teeth snapped at his fingers.

'Amy! Door!'

Amy dashed to the doors and hauled them open. The 'meteorite' had sprouted dozens of tiny legs and was starting to feel its way experimentally around the TARDIS floor. The Doctor took a step back, and then took a running kick at the gnashing pebble.

The toe of his boot connected with a satisfying clunk and the pebble sailed out through the open doors like a football through a goalmouth. Amy slammed the doors shut.

'What on Earth was that?'

'I don't know.' The Doctor raced back to the TARDIS console, staring in concern at an image of a planet on the scanner screen. 'But they are heading straight for that colony.'

Rory frowned. 'But that meteorite storm we flew through must have been huge. That would mean that there are…'

The Doctor looked at him gravely.

'Billions of them.'

CHAPTER 2
THE COLONY

Dawn was breaking over the Xirrinda Wildlife Preserve when a new noise joined the mews and cackles of the local wildlife. With a groaning rasp that drowned out everything else, the TARDIS shimmered into view.

Almost as soon as it was solid the doors crashed open and the Doctor emerged into the morning light in a whirl of arms and legs, intently studying the readings on his sonic screwdriver. Amy and Rory followed him out into the dawn, looking in bemusement at their new surroundings.

They had landed in what looked like a cross between a small airport departure lounge and a bus station; a wide, open concourse scattered with chairs and benches, bordered by a glass wall that looked out over a sweeping expanse of trees and grassland. Everything looked as if it had been built in a hurry. The twenty or thirty stalls and cafes that were scattered around the other walls looked as though they had been built from cargo containers of some kind. In amongst them were coloured booths and souvenir stalls, their yawning owners starting to set up shop for the day. Dozens of modern looking tour coaches were lined up in neat lines at one end of the building, the words 'Galactic Safari' emblazoned in colourful letters on their sides. Outside, a short distance from the terminal, a number of sleek shuttlecraft sat on a dust-strewn landing pad, their metal hulls gleaming in the early morning sun.

'Not exactly high-tech is it?' Rory was unimpressed.

'New colony,' said the Doctor, glancing around quickly. 'Probably only established in the last year or two. They're trying to get themselves established as a tourist destination by the look of things. Temporary buildings built from the colony ships whilst they wait for the engineering firms to move in and start properly.' He looked at Rory sternly. 'Very clever people these early planetary colonists. Your descendants – well, not yours directly, but your species. You should be proud of them.'

Rory flushed. 'I just meant that they don't look very well equipped to deal with hordes of small toothy monsters.'

'No…' The Doctor spun around taking in his surroundings. 'They don't, do they? I'd better have a quick word with someone in charge. Here…' He tossed a small bag to Rory. 'Local currency. Lots of nice t-shirts on the stand over there. Buy yourself some clean things.'

With that he turned and hurried across the concourse to a door marked 'Administration', vanishing inside with a cheery wave.

Amy watched him go, shaking her head. 'Typical.' She took the bag from Rory and weighed it in her hand, feeling the coins chink inside it. 'Still, if he's given us pocket money then we might as well go off and spend it.'

With that she hooked her arm into Rory's and dragged him towards one of the colourful stalls.

The Doctor entered a small reception area. A young woman was busying herself with a bundle of files on the far side of the room. The Doctor looked around. A sign reading 'Warden's Office' pointed to a small door. Slipping through the reception area as quietly as possible, the Doctor pushed open the door and bounded up the stairs, emerging into a modest control room. A man was hunched over the consoles, poking at the buttons.

'About time. We've been without long range scanners for nearly a hour…'

His face fell as he turned to look at the Doctor. 'Oh, you're not Thornton….'

'No.' The Doctor shook his head. 'I'm afraid not. I was hoping to speak to someone in charge…'

'That would be me then,' said the man, extending a tanned hand. 'I'm the warden here. Casper Van Goole.'

The Doctor shook the proffered hand.

'I'm the Doctor…'

'Doctor, eh?' Van Goole frowned. 'Shouldn't you be out on the savannah with the rest of the safari?'

'Safari… right.' The Doctor nodded, recalling the coaches in the car park. 'I'm afraid that I'm not part of any safari. My companions and I were just passing and we think that you may have a problem.'

'You're right there.' Van Goole gestured at the console. 'Can't get a blessed reading from any of them. Communications are down too. Been trying to reach the hotel complex for nearly an hour.'

The Doctor hurried over to the console.

'That's not good, not good at all.'

He whipped out his sonic screwdriver and waved it over the console, peering in concern at the read-outs. 'Same as the TARDIS...' he murmured. 'Massive gravitational distortion and disruption to the magnetic field...'

He spun around to face the warden. 'Mr Van Goole, this safari, popular is it? Lots of people?'

Van Goole nodded. 'Two dozen families out at the hotel, plus a school party, just arrived.'

'Then we need to get out to that hotel, very, very quickly.'

'Now?' Van Goole said in surprise.

'Now.' The Doctor's tone was grim. 'You and me, Mr Van Goole. You have transport?'

Van Goole nodded. 'Yes, but...'

'Of course you do. Wouldn't be much of a safari if you didn't have transport. Come along. No time to lose.'

The Doctor bounded from the control room, a confused Van Goole following after him.

In the terminal Rory followed Amy as she wandered from stall to stall, picking up t-shirts and examining them, then moving on to the next stall. Rory sighed. It was always this way when they went shopping. Why did girls always take so long?

As they approached the last stall in the row, a gangly boy stood up from behind the plastic counter. He was tall, very tall, and as they got closer Rory suddenly realised that he wasn't remotely human. He was humanoid, but stick thin, with large, cat-like eyes. His skin was the colour of teak, and as they neared the stall Rory could see that he had a second joint halfway along his forearm. As the two of them approached, he smiled widely.

'Hi. Welcome to Attar's.' He spread his arms wide, gesturing to the colourful garments spread out across the stand, the extra joint in his arm giving him a strange, insect-like look. 'Anything you like the look of?'

Rory still found that he needed time to adjust to the very fact of different life forms, but Amy seemed totally unfazed. She rummaged through the shirts on the stand as if they were at the local shopping centre rather than a souvenir stall on an alien planet. 'These are great.'

Attar grinned. 'Thanks. I'm hoping to get some of the off-worlders to take some home with them. If I can sell enough then perhaps I can get out of here one day.'

'You don't like it here?' Amy plucked a shirt from the pile and held it up into the light, examining the pattern.

Attar shrugged. 'It's ok, but it's dull. Nothing ever happens here.'

'I know that feeling. Believe me, compared to Leadworth this place is positively buzzing!' Amy held the shirt up against Rory's chest.

'Great. Bit baggy, but it does the job.'

'Are you sure?' Rory stared down at the tangle of geometric lines and swirling squiggles that now adorned his chest. 'Seems a bit colourful for me.'

'No, it looks good on you,' said Attar encouragingly. 'It's one of my most popular designs.'

'You do these yourself?' asked Amy. 'What are the designs based on?'

Attar shrugged. 'Just stuff. Patterns and drawings from the legends that we are taught about when we're children.'

'Legends?'

'Tribal stuff, that's all. Stories that the old folk

keep telling us are important to remember.'

'Cool. We'll take two. That one for Rory…' she tugged another shirt from the pile. 'And this one for me.'

Amy rummaged in the bag of change that the Doctor had given them, pulling out a couple of large, coppery, octagonal coins.

'That enough?'

Attar took the coins. 'Perfect.' He stuffed them into his pocket.

Rory had a sneaking suspicion that they had just been overcharged, but he wasn't about to start an argument. He shrugged off his old, mud-splattered shirt and slipped the clean t-shirt over his head. Amy nodded approvingly at him. 'Right. I'm going to change. Won't be a jiffy.'

She gave Rory a peck on the cheek and headed across the concourse to the toilets.

Rory was aware of Attar's cat-like eyes watching him.

'You part of the safari?' he asked, curiously.

Rory shook his head. 'We were… just passing. On our way to a party.' He didn't think he should mention the real reason for their arrival. Not yet.

'Really…' Attar looked at him strangely. 'If you find a party of any kind round here, let me know.'

The noise of an engine made them both look round. Another coach was pulling up into its bay. It came to a standstill and the doors hissed open. Dozens of noisy children spilled out across the concourse, running over to the huge windows and pressing their faces to the glass, staring out at the savannah, chattering excitedly.

Attar rubbed his hands expectantly. 'More eager punters.'

As Attar hurried forward to greet the new arrivals, Amy emerged from the toilets. She caught sight of the children and Rory could see the worried look in her eye.

'We need to let these people know what's

coming,' she whispered.

Rory nodded. He just hoped that the Doctor had a plan.

The Doctor and Van Goole emerged from the terminal into the warm, dry air of the car park. A bright red open-topped vehicle that looked like a cross between a mini and a hovercraft was parked in an official bay. The warden clambered into the driving seat.

'Hop in.'

The Doctor swung his legs over the sill and squeezed his lanky frame into the passenger seat. Van Goole slid an electronic key into the dashboard and thumbed the ignition. The engine made a choking cough, then died.

'Blast!' Van Goole tried to start the hover car again. 'What is going on with the electrics in this place today?'

The Doctor had a nasty suspicion that he knew

the answer to that. 'Hang on a mo.' He delved into his jacket pocket for his sonic screwdriver and pulled open an inspection panel on the dashboard. He thrust the sonic into the workings. 'Try it now', he said, raising his voice above the warbling whine.

Van Goole turned the key and the engine sprung into life with a whirr. The vehicle lifted a few feet off the ground and with a practised spin of the wheel, Van Goole backed it out of the parking space.

'You're a handy man to have around, Doctor.' He grinned. 'I should keep you on as my scientific advisor.'

The hover car sped out past the terminal building. The Doctor could see Amy and Rory staring at them in surprise as they shot past the window.

'Won't be long, Pond!' shouted the Doctor, giving Amy a thumbs up. 'See if you can find out what the transport situation is like!'

With that, Van Goole stepped on the accelerator and the little car surged forward.

Amy put her hands on her hips and stared through the glass in frustration as the car vanished towards the distant horizon in a cloud of dust.

'Typical,' she muttered.

Rory shook his head in disbelief. 'Has he just gone off and left us stranded here?'

'Off on a jolly whilst we have to do all the hard work, as usual.'

'And what does he mean, find out what the transport situation is like? We've got the TARDIS and there are all those shuttlecraft...'

'And he knows that, so I'm guessing that there's something he's not telling us.'

'Again, as usual.' Rory sighed.

'Well, there's no point moaning about it. He's given us a job, so let's get on with it.' Amy looked around the concourse. There were doors and corridors everywhere: signs pointing out the visitor centre, restaurants, toilets, plus a dozen more that stated 'Official Personnel Only'.

'You go that way, I'll go this way. Meet you back here in fifteen minutes.'

Amy strode off across the concourse. She just hoped that the Doctor wasn't going to be long. There was a strange feeling in the air, as if a storm was brewing, and Amy had a horrible suspicion that the meteorite shower wasn't far behind.

Matty George and Kevin Arkwright stepped gratefully from the coach into the air-conditioned cool of the building, looking around eagerly. They were both part of a field trip to Xirrinda organised by their school. So far, however, the trip had been a disappointment to both of them. They had thought that they were going to see wild animals and primitive tribesmen armed with fearsome weapons, but so far they had spent most of their time studying some paintings inside a damp old cave. The only animals they had seen were beetles and the odd bird.

Kevin's face fell as he took in their surroundings. 'What a dump.'

'Oh, I dunno.' Matty looked over at where Attar was waving animatedly at them. 'There might be some cool native stuff on some of those stands.'

'Like what?' sniffed Kevin. All he could see were crummy t-shirts.

'I dunno. Masks. Spears. Shrunken heads…'

'Can I remind you that you are here to gather research material for your mid-term exams, not to collect tacky souvenirs.'

Both boys spun around to see Mr Cain glaring at them. He had been a last minute replacement after their regular history teacher had gone down with a bad attack of flu the day before they were due to leave. Cain was a tall, thin-faced man with a permanent frown, and none of their class liked him. He was grumpy, impatient and had a nasty temper. They had even heard some of the other teachers muttering about him under their breath.

'Your task today, as I recall, is to gather information on the history of the local native population. I expect to see your reports at the end of the day.'

Matty wanted to point out that looking at native artefacts might be the best way of learning about their history, but both he and Kevin had already fallen foul of Cain a couple of times on this trip. Rather than risk another confrontation the boys nodded and hurried to join their classmates.

The Doctor was silent on the journey towards the wildlife preserve, his mind whirring. Rory had been right when he had said that the colony was not well equipped to deal with any kind of disaster situation, and the Doctor had a nasty suspicion that disaster was exactly what was about to happen.

As the hover car sped through the dry bush land, the engine continued to make unhealthy sounding noises. The Doctor stopped his musings and continued to nursemaid the car. They zoomed up a steep rise, emerging onto the top of a long narrow ridge overlooking the savannah. Suddenly Van Goole brought the vehicle to a stop.

'What the devil?'

The Doctor stood up in his seat, leaning on the windshield and pulling out his binoculars. Ahead of them, a dark cloud spread across the horizon and the air was filled with a buzzing drone, like the sound from a hive of bees.

'It's them...' The Doctor's voice was grim. The creatures from the asteroid storm had landed. The Doctor turned to Van Goole.

'We're too late. Everyone in that hotel is dead.'

CHAPTER 3
SURVIVOR

Van Goole stared at him blankly, unwilling to believe what he was hearing.

'What are they?'

'At a guess, a parasitic species of some kind, drifting between planets, drawn by gravity. They arrive, rain down on the surface, strip it bare…' The Doctor handed him the binoculars. 'There must be tens of billions of them in that storm, and they're coming this way. We've got to get back to the colony.'

'No, wait.' Van Goole caught his arm. 'There's

something down there!'

The Doctor followed his gaze. A brightly-coloured shape gleamed amongst the dry brush. The Doctor snatched the binoculars from Van Goole and adjusted the focus.

A jeep was wedged into a dry creek-bed, one wheel jutting out at a sharp angle, the windshield cracked. As the Doctor peered at it he could see faint movement from within.

'There's someone alive!'

Van Goole tried to start the hover car but the engine just clicked and whined protestingly.

'It won't start!' he cried.

'Keep trying!' The Doctor leapt from the car and bounded down the steep slope towards the crashed jeep, arms and legs flailing wildly. The noise from the approaching swarm was deafening, the whistle and thump as more and more fell from the sky, the clacking and snapping of millions of pairs of teeth, and the frightened cries of the animals driven into a wild stampede by the approaching monsters.

The Doctor dodged out of the way as a pair of gazelle-like creatures thundered past him. He tumbled into the dry creek-bed and hauled open the door of the jeep. Sprawled in a heap on the back seat was a young girl, a livid bruise on her forehead from where she had crashed into the back of the driver's seat. For a second the Doctor was confused. Where was the driver? Then he noticed the gleaming autopilot controls. The car had been on automatic control. Someone had obviously tried to get the girl away from danger, but somehow the vehicle had gone off course, either because it had been trying to avoid one of the frightened animals or because the computer had been affected by the interference.

'Doctor!' From the distance came a cry of alarm from Van Goole. 'Get out of there!' Something hard banged down on the roof. Jolted into action, the Doctor scooped the girl up into his arms, struggled out of the creek-bed and made for the ridge. From behind him came the relentless clattering of billions of feet and the chomp, chomp, chomp of teeth. The Doctor didn't look back. He ran.

All around him tiny missiles rained down onto the dry earth. The Doctor stumbled forward, kicking the creatures out of the way before they cracked open and got their bearings. Finally, he reached the top of the rise, gratefully letting Van Goole take the girl from him.

'Was there anyone else?' asked Van Goole.

The Doctor shook his head. 'We've got to go. Now!' he said breathlessly.

Van Goole gestured helplessly at the controls. 'Nothing's working!'

The Doctor leant forward, nose pressed into the controls. 'Somehow the creatures are generating a massive amount of gravitational and electromagnetic interference. It's shutting down anything electrical, but if I can persuade the computer that it can run the engine from sonic impulses instead...'

There was a sharp bang as something hard bounced off the bonnet of the hover car.

Van Goole watched in horror as the 'pebble' bounced off into the dirt, then cracked open with a hiss.

'Doctor...'

'Nearly there!'

More and more pebble creatures rained down around them.

'We're not going to make it!'

'Oh yes we are!' The engine roared into life just as another pebble monster shattered the windshield and landed in the foot-well. The Doctor tossed it out of the car with a flick of his wrist. 'Go, Van Goole! Go!'

The warden stamped on the throttle and the

hover car surged forwards.

Amy knew that something was wrong as soon as the little red hover car pulled up outside the terminal. She raised her hand to her mouth as the Doctor struggled from the passenger seat with a limp body in his arms.

'Oh, no.'

The Doctor hurried up the stairs and into the terminal building, Van Goole holding the door open for him.

'Rory!' shouted the Doctor. 'I need you over here, quickly.'

Amy and Rory raced over to where the Doctor was carefully laying the body on one of the benches. It was a young girl, no more than ten years old.

Amy looked down at her pale face in despair. 'Is she...?'

'No.' Rory was checking her pulse. 'She's fine.' He examined the bruise on her forehead. 'It looks like she's got a mild concussion. Is there somewhere where we can take her?'

The Doctor shot a look at Van Goole. He nodded.

'There's a small medical room. Not much, I'm afraid. It's this way.'

Rory and Van Goole gently lifted the girl between them and carried her across the concourse. Amy made to follow but the Doctor stopped her.

'Did you have any luck?'

Despite herself Amy had to smile.

'I think that you'd better come and look.'

The two of them hurried across to a set of double doors marked 'No Admittance'. Pushing them open, Amy led the Doctor onto a wide platform. It was gloomy and musty, and smelled of engine oil. As the Doctor's eyes became accustomed to the dark he could make out a long metal shape looming over him.

His face cracked into an enormous smile.

'Oh, you beauty.'

'They're coming!'

The girl sat bolt upright in the small bed, her eyes wide with fear. Rory hurried over to her bedside. 'Hey, hey, hey. It's alright. You're safe.'

The girl looked around in alarm, her panic slowly fading as she took in her surroundings.

'Are they here?' she asked, her voice wavering.

'Those rock things?' Rory shook his head. 'No.'

'What's your name?' asked Van Goole, gently.

'Gellen. Gellen Jenkins.'

'What happened, Gellen?'

The girl looked at him with frightened eyes. 'They fell from the sky like rain. They just kept coming. They were so fast. They killed everything.'

Van Goole gave Rory a worried look. He turned to the console. 'Let's see if we can find out what we are up against.'

Rory frowned. 'I thought that nothing was working?'

'Nothing is working *well,* but I just need to get a signal from one of our weather radar satellites. They might be far enough up to avoid any interference.'

He settled into a chair in front of a console, manipulating the controls with practised hands. Screens flickered into life showing an image of a pale, yellow globe. 'Bingo!' Van Goole twisted a dial and the image zoomed closer.

'Good God.' The warden's voice dropped to a whisper.

Rory peered at the screen. Even though he didn't recognise the shape of the continents and oceans it was obvious that he was looking at an image of the planet from orbit. Unlike Earth the planet was a mass of browns and yellows. On one side of the screen was a fuzzy grey mass, flickering like static. It covered a huge area, its front edge rippling and moving slowly across the landmass. The enormous scale of the meteorite swarm suddenly became clear.

Van Goole looked up at Rory with frightened eyes.

'I think that you'd better get the Doctor.'

Amy watched as the Doctor scampered all over the train like a child with a new toy. She had been in a deserted office on the upper story of the terminal building when she had noticed the single gleaming rail stretching off towards the horizon. Following it back she had discovered the platform and the gleaming train inside.

It was a monorail – three cylindrical carriages linked by flexible corridors, a blister-like cab on one end.

'This is perfect, Pond. Totally perfect.' The Doctor beamed down at her. 'I always wanted to be a train driver when I was a boy.'

'Here! What the devil do you two think you're playing at?'

The gruff voice made Amy start. A stocky man with a salt and pepper beard was glaring at them from the doorway. The Doctor scrambled down from the cab and hurried over.

'Mr Thornton, I presume. Just the man I wanted to meet. Good with trains are you? Silly question. You're an engineer on an outer rim planet, so of course you're good with trains. Now then, how long will it take you to get this lovely machine ready to run?'

'This old thing?' Thornton gave a coughing laugh. 'It's not been used in over a year. You'd have to be a genius to get this thing fired up and ready to go in less than three or four days.'

'Well, it's a good thing I am a genius, Mr Thornton, because you and I have got less than three or four hours.'

CHAPTER 4
THE DOCTOR TAKES CHARGE

Matty and Kevin were pottering around the stalls keeping well out of the way of Cain when a piercing whistle rang out through the air. Both boys turned to see a gangly man hop up onto a bench in the middle of the terminal, a pretty red-haired girl following after him. As they watched, the man put his fingers in his mouth and gave another piercing whistle.

'If I could have your attention please!' he bellowed.

The two boys exchanged a curious glance and

then hurried forward to see what was going on. The man on the bench had now attracted a small crowd, mostly made up of other children from the field trip, plus a few of the locals. A puzzled murmur rippled through the crowd.

'Hello. I'm the Doctor.' The man beamed at them, rubbing his hands together as he turned in a slow circle, taking in the sea of puzzled faces.

'Now from the look of things most of you are probably here for a nice holiday, looking to get away from it all, or a school trip to learn all about an alien world. Well, I'm afraid that everything is cancelled. We need to get you all away from here as quickly as possible. Any questions?'

There was a moment's stunned silence, then the square exploded into a frenzied chatter of voices. Suddenly Matty could hear a tinny voice cutting over the din. 'Let me through, come on, clear a path here.'

Matty turned to Kevin and grinned. 'Here

comes trouble.'

A small chubby man pushed through the crowds towards the Doctor, his face red with rage. It was Professor Willard, their head teacher. He stormed up to the Doctor, glaring at him angrily.

'What's all this nonsense about cancellation? I've got rooms booked at the hotel.'

The Doctor hopped down off the bench. 'Well I'm very sorry, Mr…?'

'Professor! Professor Willard, from the Outer Planet's School's Association. We've got a four day field trip booked…'

'Well, that's lovely, but I'm afraid that I've got more to worry about than whether you got the right rooms in your hotel. We have a dangerous situation…'

'Well, that's your problem,' Willard cut across him. 'We have a very strict timetable and it cannot be disrupted.'

'I don't think you quite understand, Mr

Willard…' The Doctor tried to explain but Willard was in no mood to listen.

'It's Professor Willard, and I made it quite clear when I made this booking that we were working on a tight budget and a carefully balanced schedule. I was assured by Mr Van Goole that everything would be in order…'

'And as I am trying to explain…'

'Where is the warden, anyway? Are you even part of his team? You certainly don't dress like one of his people.'

'Professor Willard,' snapped the Doctor. 'Shut up!'

Matty and Kevin's jaws dropped open in shock. No one ever talked to Willard like that. The little Professor looked as though he had been slapped. A silence descended across the crowd, and all eyes turned to the Doctor as he leaned forward.

'The last thing I need at the moment is someone arguing with me every step of the way. I need you to listen and I need you to do exactly as I tell you. We need to evacuate this building and we need to do it quickly. If you will come with me I will explain everything. In the meantime your staff need to start getting these children ready to leave. Do you understand?'

Willard nodded weakly. Matty had never seen him speechless before. He stifled a giggle. This was fantastic.

The Doctor turned to the red-haired girl standing behind him. 'Amy, see what you can do to help. Tell the locals what's going on, but quietly. We don't want to start a panic.'

The girl – Amy – nodded and hurried off.

Matty and Kevin exchanged a puzzled glance. Their field trip had just got considerably more interesting.

Amy hurried over to where Attar was watching with interest from his stall. There was amusement in the tall alien's eyes as he chinked a pile of gleaming coins in his hands. 'Your friend has quite a way of making an impression. I should get him to do some sales pitches for me! What was he going on about, anyway?'

Amy lowered her voice and explained quickly and quietly about the creatures and the approaching swarm. As she did so all amusement drained from Attar's face and his body stiffened.

'That's impossible. It's just a story…'

Quickly he thrust the coins into the till and grabbed a coat from the stand.

'Where are you going?' asked Amy. 'You can't just leave! We've got to help with the preparations to evacuate.'

Attar shook his head. 'I can't.'

'You can't just run off!'

'You don't understand. My people, my tribe. They live in a reservation out on the savannah. I've got to warn them.'

With that he ran off across the concourse, with long, loping strides. Amy watched him go in despair. She had been confident that the train had more than enough space for everyone in the colony, but if there was a whole tribe that they had to rescue as well... She turned and hurried over to the administration office to tell the Doctor the bad news.

Willard sat at the conference table, his face pale with shock as the Doctor explained the nature of the threat that they faced.

'So you see, Professor,' said the Doctor quietly. 'We have a bit of a problem.'

The Professor nodded.

The Doctor was peering intently at the radar images on the screen. He tapped a long finger against the glass. 'This is very strange, the area behind the creatures appears to be hard, smooth, reflective, as if they're leaving something behind them, a trail of some kind.' He adjusted the controls and the picture zoomed closer. Sunlight glared off something hard.

'It looks like metal,' ventured Rory.

'Yes. It's as if the creatures are depositing a metal coating behind them, the same way that a snail deposits slime. They arrive, eat everything in their path and then…'

'Leave metal poo behind?' Rory frowned. 'Why?'

'I don't know.' The Doctor started to pace around the room. 'There's something not right here, something I'm missing…'

'That's all very well, Doctor,' said Van Goole. 'But we have to get away from here. You say that the shuttles are not an option, so what are we going to do?'

'The monorail,' said the Doctor firmly. 'I'm assuming it was built to ferry tourists here from some larger colony, yes? So it must run back to a major transportation hub.'

Van Goole nodded. 'It's an express line over to Ortagon City on the east coast. It was meant to be part of the safari experience. Originally it had a branch line that went out to the caves, but we had some opposition from the locals over that.' Van Goole shrugged. 'It didn't prove as popular as we hoped so it doesn't get used very often. The occasional private booking, other than that we use it as a back-up if the shuttles are grounded.'

'Then what we do is this. Get everyone onto the train, get to the city as fast as possible. As soon as we are a good distance from the creatures then we should be able to re-establish communications and arrange a full-scale evacuation of the planet.'

'The entire planet?' Van Goole looked shocked. 'That's nearly eight million colonists! Do you have any idea what it is that you are suggesting?'

'I know exactly what I am suggesting, Mr Van Goole. If we can't escape and warn people what is coming, then eight million people are going to die. These creatures are not going to stop until they have ravaged the entire planet. At present I can't think of anything that I can do to stop them, so all I can suggest is that we run.'

'Run.' Rory looked at him sternly. 'That's the plan? Run?'

The Doctor looked flustered. 'It's not the cleverest plan that I've ever come up with, I'll admit, but it's the best I can do in the circumstances. If I come up with anything better then I'll let you know.'

To his credit, Van Goole didn't argue. He turned to his frightened secretary. 'Ellie, would you inform all senior staff of what is happening and assist Mr Thornton with whatever he needs to get preparations underway. Professor Willard, will you ensure that all the children are told to co-operate with my staff?'

Willard nodded.

'Splendid.' The Doctor smiled. 'Everything under control.'

The door crashed open and Amy burst into the room. 'I think that we may have a problem.'

The Doctor emerged into the daylight with a face like thunder, Van Goole, Amy and Rory following in his wake.

'So when were you going to tell me about the settlement, Van Goole?' snapped the Doctor angrily.

'Doctor, my responsibility is to my people first,' blustered the warden.

'And what about Attar's people? Who takes responsibility for them?'

'The train has barely got enough capacity as it is!'

'So you were just going to leave them?'

'I…' Van Goole faltered. 'I don't know.'

The Doctor stopped, his tone softening. 'Look, things are bad, I know, but are we really going to let an entire tribe of people get wiped out because we can't find an extra couple of seats on a train?'

Van Goole shook his head.

The Doctor smiled. 'Good man. Now where is this settlement?'

Van Goole nodded at a dirt track leading out towards the savannah. 'Follow the road for about a mile. You can't miss it.' He tossed the Doctor his keys. 'Take the hover car. We'll start getting things ready at this end.'

The Doctor nodded and hurried towards the car. As he reached it he realised that Amy and Rory were following him. As he opened his mouth to object, Amy held up her hand and glared at him sternly.

'Before you start, no, we are not staying behind

to help load boxes whilst you vanish off into the distance again. Don't even bother arguing.'

The Doctor closed his mouth and shot a glance at Rory.

Rory shrugged. He knew from experience that once Amy had made up her mind there was no point in trying to change it.

'All right.' The Doctor nodded reluctantly. 'But be careful. And no wandering off!'

'As if!'

The Doctor clambered into the car, Amy and Rory squeezing into the passenger seat alongside him.

'Hold on tight!' said the Doctor, thrusting the sonic screwdriver into the dashboard once more.

The little car shot forward in a cloud of dust.

The journey to the reservation only took a few minutes. Despite the coming danger, Amy took a moment to take in the experience of being on another planet again. It still surprised her how quickly she had come to treat everything as ordinary and everyday. Sometimes she wished that she could experience everything with the same surprised wonder that her husband did. She glanced across at where Rory was chewing his nails nervously. Perhaps terrified wonder was a better description. She gave his arm a gentle squeeze.

He smiled at her. Despite the dangers that they faced, she was glad that he was there to share all of this with her.

The Doctor hadn't said a word since they had left town. That was a bad sign. For him not to confront things with his usual cheery bravado meant that things were serious.

As the hover car rounded a bend, a cluster of thatched shacks came into view. The Doctor brought the car to a halt and the three of them clambered out. The village was deserted. The Doctor crossed to where the remains of a fire smouldered in the dusty earth. A metal pot hung from a hook over the embers. He turned around slowly, taking in every detail.

'How many people were meant to be here?' asked Amy.

'About seventy families, according to Mr Van Goole,' answered the Doctor.

'Well they left in a hurry.'

'Yes,' the Doctor knelt in the dirt by a fenced area, examining a jumble of tracks. 'And they took all their pack animals with them as well.'

'So are you saying that they already knew what was coming?' asked Rory, puzzled.

'Yes,' muttered the Doctor. 'Somehow they realised the danger that they were in and they left to find somewhere safe…'

'Amy?' A voice rang out through the still air.

The three of them turned to see a figure emerging from one of the larger huts.

'Friend of yours?' The Doctor raised a quizzical

eyebrow.

'It's Attar,' said Amy, hurrying over to him.

The young stallholder looked completely shell-shocked.

'They've all gone.'

'They left you behind?'

'They've taken everything. Just as the legend said…'

'Attar.' The Doctor's voice was suddenly urgent. 'Your people. They've encountered these things before, yes? They had some plan. Somewhere safe. Do you know where they've gone?'

'I thought that it was just a story. Something to scare children…'

'What did they know?'

'The Rain of Terror…'

'Tell me!'

'I'll show you.' Attar led the Doctor back into the hut. Amy followed them.

The interior of the hut was gloomy, with a smell

like incense sticks. It reminded Amy of the local church in Leadworth, and she suddenly realised that the building was indeed a holy place of some kind. Light filtered in from a high window in the centre of the roof and rows of low stools circled a low altar.

The Doctor and Attar were standing at the altar, talking in low voices. Amy hurried over, trying to catch what they were saying.

'This shrine contained the history of my people,' explained Attar. 'Paintings and murals that the old men used to teach the young ones about the story of who we are and where we came from…'

'And every one of these pictures has gone?'

Attar nodded. 'I have never known a time when they have not been here. For them to have been removed…'

He trailed off.

'This history, you are all taught it as children?' The Doctor kept his voice gentle, but Amy could tell he was desperate to find some clue that might give him an edge in the battle that they faced.

Attar looked at him in despair. 'We are, but I never paid it any attention. I was young and headstrong. I thought that they were nothing but old stories told by old men. They seemed to have so little meaning to me. I thought that we should be looking to the future, not dragging the past along with us.'

The Doctor smiled sadly. 'I know.' Amy could see that a part of him knew only too well what Attar meant, but it was not the news that he had hoped to hear.

'Do you have any idea of where they might have gone?'

'No!'

'Attar, think! These stories, these legends, they must have been drummed into you as a boy. I know what teachers are like. Even if you weren't interested something must have sunk in. Somewhere in your subconscious you must know where they might have gone.'

Attar's face creased with effort. 'I'm trying to remember, but...'

At that moment Rory backed slowly in through the doorway to the shrine.

'Er, Doctor...' he stammered.

'Not now, Rory!' Amy waved her hand at him impatiently. 'This is important!'

'No, Amy, I really think that this might be important too!'

Amy, Attar and the Doctor turned to see two dark shapes slinking in through the doorway after Rory. They were long and slender, their bodies covered with slick black fur. They moved slowly, hugging the ground, large wet noses twitching constantly.

'What are they?' whispered Amy as one of the creatures lifted its head and snarled, revealing rows of small, sharp teeth.

Attar took a step back, paling visibly.

'Sharkwolves.'

CHAPTER 5
RUNNING OUT OF TIME

The snarling creatures sniffed at the air, moving their heads to and fro as they tried to locate their prey.

'I don't suppose these things are vegetarian, by any chance?' said Rory, gulping.

'Attar,' hissed the Doctor. 'I need you to tell me everything that you can about these creatures, and quickly!'

'They're hunters, pack animals. But they never usually come out in the day, and never usually come this close to the reservation.'

'They're being driven towards us by the advancing swarm. That means that they're frightened and hungry. Not a good combination. But you said that they're nocturnal?'

Attar nodded.

'Then that gives us a chance. Their vision is adapted for low light, so they're probably nearly blind in daylight. We've got to get back out into the daylight. Now, I need everyone to stay quiet and move slowly back towards the wall. Keep the altar between us and them.'

The four of them started to make their way slowly back towards the rear of the temple. Amy was suddenly very aware of every cracking twig under foot, of every rustle of clothing.

The Sharkwolves continued to slink around the edges of the shrine, sharp claws occasionally slashing at each other, hissing and snarling. As they moved slowly around the wall, Amy and the others kept on the opposite side of the hut, hugging the wall. The door was tantalisingly close. Amy could see the Doctor reaching for the keys to the hover car in his pocket.

'When I say run,' he whispered. 'Run.'

Amy tensed herself, ready for the final dash, when there was a sudden snarl as one of the Sharkwolves spotted them.

'Run!' cried the Doctor.

The four of them hurled themselves out of the door and into the sunlight. As they did so, Amy became aware of something huge thundering out of the bush. For one horrible moment she thought that more of the Sharkwolves had been waiting for them, but as she started to make sense of the chaos in front of her, she realised that it was a herd of gazelle-like creatures, mad with fear, crashing through the village in a blind panic. Behind them, the Sharkwolves launched themselves out of the shrine at the panicked animals, their snarls and hisses terrifyingly loud.

'It's a Trinto herd!' Attar had to shout to make himself heard above the din.

'We'll have time for the natural history lesson later!' bellowed the Doctor. 'Keep moving!'

Grateful for the unexpected distraction, the four of them hurled themselves into the hover car and the Doctor coaxed the engine into life. As they sped from the village, Amy could hear nothing but the agonised screams of the Trinto and the triumphant cries of the Sharkwolves as they gorged themselves on their prey.

It was what lay in store for all of them if they didn't get away before the swarm arrived.

When they arrived back at the terminal building, everything was bustling with activity. The shutter wall alongside the train platform had been opened up and a steady stream of food and medical supplies was being loaded onto the train.

Van Goole hurried over as they came to a halt.

'I thought you'd have a crowd in tow.' He looked at Attar, puzzled. 'No one else would come with you?'

'No one else was there,' said the Doctor. 'Gone, vamoosed.'

He quickly explained to the warden what they had found at the reservation. Van Goole listened, a flicker of hope on his face. 'And you think that they've found somewhere to go that they can hide from these things? Somewhere safe?'

The Doctor nodded. 'I'm certain of it. Now I've just got to work out where.'

Van Goole sighed. 'Well let me know when you work it out! In the meantime, Thornton would like a word with you and I'd like to borrow Rory.'

'Me?' Rory looked surprised. 'What do you want with me?'

'We've had a slight accident. One of the children... a broken arm I think...'

'I'm just a nurse, you know.....'

'Our medical staff was small, and almost all of them were over at the hotel when the creatures attacked. That means they're all dead.'

Rory nodded.

'I'll do what I can.'

'How's it going, Mr Thornton?'

Thornton looked up in relief as the Doctor clambered up into the cabin.

'Doctor, I hope you weren't lying when you said that you were a genius.'

'Why?' asked the Doctor. 'What's wrong?'

Thornton put down a greasy wrench and wiped his hands on his overalls.

'I'll show you.'

He ducked through a narrow hatchway into the main engine compartment of the train, the Doctor squeezing in behind him.

'I've done as you said and disconnected most of the computer auto-controls. That means I can control the throttle and brakes manually. The main reactor will run on hydrogen fuel cells from the main colony generator, but the problem is here…'

Thornton tapped a console.

'I need the computer to regulate the boiler pressure. No computer, no temperature control. Too cold and we stop moving, too hot and we blow the main engine.'

The Doctor peered at the read-outs. 'How critical is the margin?'

Thornton shrugged. 'Ten degrees either way. If there was more time I could rig up a mechanical regulator, but if those things are getting as close as you say…'

'Don't you worry about it, Mr Thornton.' The Doctor beamed at him. 'I think I've got a perfect replacement for the computer!'

Matty and Kevin sat in the stifling warmth of the

tour bus watching as teachers bustled around them. Willard had sat them all down and told them about the hordes of hungry creatures that were approaching, and of the plan to try and evacuate everyone by train.

Some of the other kids had started to cry: some of the teachers too. Matty just felt a kind of numb shock. It was as if he was watching events unfold on a news report, and the fact that it was actually happening to him didn't feel real somehow.

'Are you frightened?' Kevin was looking at him.

'Yes. I guess so.'

'What do you think will happen if they can't get that old train working?'

'They will. Besides, they're bound to have radioed Ortagon City for help. There's probably a shuttle on the way already.'

Kevin shook his head. 'I heard Willard talking to the other teachers. These creatures that are coming are doing something that affects machinery. That's why we're trying to use the train.'

'Won't that be affected too?'

Kevin shrugged. 'I guess not.'

There was a sudden bustle from the front of the bus and the gangly man that had told Mr Willard to shut up bounded into the aisle between the seats.

'Hello. Me again. The Doctor.' He waved cheerily. 'Anyone here ever wanted to help drive a train?'

The kids all looked at him blankly.

'Um, no, I really mean it. We need two of you to help. It's important. I need two of you who can be trusted. The lives of everyone in this colony depend on it.'

There was a shocked silence for a moment, and then Matty raised his hand.

'You can't be serious!'

Thornton and Van Goole looked at the Doctor

as if he was mad.

'I'm completely serious. Why, what's the problem?'

'But they're kids!'

'So?'

'We're talking about trusting the lives of everyone in this colony to two twelve year old boys.'

'Yes.'

The Doctor turned to where Matty and Kevin were standing. 'You two, you understand how important this is, don't you?'

The boys nodded.

'And you're quite clear about what I've told you needs to be done?'

The boys nodded again.

'You want us to keep an eye on these controls.' Kevin pointed at the temperature gauge. 'If it gets too high, we move this lever…'

'And if it gets too low we use this one.' Matty finished for him.

'Right.' The Doctor turned back to Van Goole

with a beaming smile. 'See?'

Van Goole shook his head. 'I can't allow it. This is madness.'

'No,' snapped the Doctor. 'It's madness to favour machines instead of people. It's madness not realising that the human brain is the most fantastic computer ever created. It's madness not trusting important things to the brightest and the best because you have decided that they are too young. You were more than happy to trust your lives to a machine that thinks with a computer chip built in a nameless factory on a distant planet by another machine. Trust me. Trust them.'

Van Goole said nothing for a moment, then nodded. 'All right, Doctor. You win.'

The Doctor grinned, then turned and winked at the two boys. 'Come on you two. Let's get you set up.'

The Doctor was watching the TARDIS being

loaded onto the train when Amy came over to his side. He smiled at her.

'Hello, Pond.'

'You're worried aren't you?' asked Amy.

The Doctor said nothing.

'Now I know you're worried. Otherwise there would have been some snappy remark telling me of your grand plan. Don't you think that the train is going to work?'

'Oh, the train is going to work fine,' said the Doctor firmly. 'Built by the Off-Planet Railroad Company, solid as a rock…'

'But…'

'But I'm only giving us a breathing space.' The Doctor looked straight at her. 'The creatures are multiplying at a frightening rate. The more they eat, the more they breed, the bigger the swarm…'

'The more severe the interference they generate.'

The Doctor nodded. 'Every hour that passes, the chances of us being able to get a ship into the air gets slimmer. When we get far enough away we have to radio the city ahead and warn them that they have to start evacuating. Immediately. If we're not fast enough crossing the desert then when we reach Ortagon city on the other side of the desert all the shuttles will be gone and we will be in exactly the same position as we are now.'

'We'd better get cracking then, eh?' Amy tried to sound braver then she felt.

In the corridor nearby, Cain listened grim-faced as the Doctor explained the situation to his young companion. He was already less than keen about the thought of escaping on an outdated, clapped-out monorail. Learning that it might only give them a few hours breathing space made him even less keen.

He chewed his lip.

The train wasn't an escape; it was only a way of delaying the inevitable. He needed another way out.

He hurried back onto the concourse, crossing to where Willard and the other teachers were busying themselves with preparations for the evacuation.

'Willard.'

The professor looked around in irritation. 'It's Professor Willard, if you don't mind. Where have you been, Julius? There's a lot to do here.'

'We need to talk.'

'We'll have plenty of time to talk when we're on the train.'

'Now.'

Cain's tone made it perfectly clear that he wasn't about to be argued with. Reluctantly Willard followed him to a side corridor.

Cain glanced over at the other teachers, checking that they were well away from any prying ears, but they were too busy with their own survival.

'We don't have time for this, Julius,' said Willard.

'Shut up and listen for a moment.'

Willard flushed. He knew that he shouldn't put up with being spoken to like this, but Julius Cain had always been a bully, right from when they had been children. He never had had the strength to stand up to him.

'These creatures – these stone things – do you know what they are?'

Willard shook his head. 'I've never come across anything like them before.'

Cain nodded. 'That's what I thought. So they'll be valuable, yes?'

Willard gave a little laugh of disbelief. 'Of all the times to think of something like…'

'Listen!' snapped Cain. 'These things are falling out of the sky. You get one of your specimen boxes and meet me at the front of the terminal building. Don't tell anyone what you're doing.'

Amongst the bustle and chaos of the evacuation the Doctor was suddenly aware of a lone figure, watching silently from a bench on one side of the terminal.

Gellen.

The Doctor crossed to her and crouched down, bringing his head level with hers. 'Are you all right?' he asked quietly.

'Are we really going to try and escape on that old train?'

The Doctor held her gaze. He had to admit that the train *did* look a little battered and old.

'Well… yes.' He tried to sound confident. 'It is a classic design.'

'Why don't we just get into the shuttles and fly away?'

'Because the creatures are generating a gravitational…' The Doctor stopped himself. 'The creatures talk to each other using gravity. And messing around with gravity near shuttlecraft is not good. Not good at all.'

'But they're fast.'

'But we'll be faster.' The Doctor caught hold

of Gellen's hands. 'Listen to me. This train is going to be the fastest thing you've ever seen. It's going to get us far away from these creatures. So far away that their gravity won't affect us any more. When we get to the city on the other side of the mountains, there will be loads of shuttles, then we'll get off this planet.'

Gellen stared at him.

'You promise?'

The Doctor grinned at her. 'Cross my hearts.'

Gellen suddenly jumped as something ran across her feet. The Doctor looked down as dozens of small rodent-like creatures bolted from a service duct and scurried away across the concourse, squeaking loudly.

The Doctor got to his feet. Through the picture window he could see a dull grey haze in the sky over the savannah and he could hear noise starting to build, like distant whispering.

He caught Gellen by the hand and pulled her

upright.

'Get to the train. Tell Mr Thornton that we need to be ready to leave. Now.'

'Is it them?' asked Gellen.

The Doctor nodded. They were out of time. The rain of terror had arrived.

CHAPTER 6
ESCAPE!

Amy watched with frightened eyes as the sky continued to darken outside the windows of the terminal building. The whispering noise was now so loud that it drowned out everything else. Behind her teachers were ushering the last of the children onto the train, whilst Van Goole's team were helping Rory set up a makeshift medical unit in the first class compartment. Amy could see Rory checking that Gellen was okay. She felt a warm glow of pride. He was brilliant with kids. He'd make a great dad one day.

The Doctor, Van Goole and Thornton were making last minute checks to the engine. Amy had overheard the engineer telling the Doctor his concerns about the weight that the train was carrying. It had far more people on-board than it had ever been designed for. What if it was too much? Amy shook her head, dismissing her fears. The Doctor wouldn't have let things get this far if he had any doubts that the train was capable of getting them all away from here.

Amy spun as something hard hit the window. As she watched there was another impact, and another. Dark shapes started to clatter against the glass. Before she even had time to cry out, there was a splintering crash and one of the glass panes exploded into a million fragments. Amy stared, horrified as dozens of small pebble-like shapes clattered to the ground. Almost immediately there was the familiar 'crack' as they split open, then the skittering of clawed feet on the terminal floor.

Amy turned and ran towards the train. 'Doctor!' she screamed.

The Doctor looked up as another of the huge picture windows cracked from the relentless impact of the falling stones.

'Come on, Pond!' cried the Doctor, grasping her by the hand and pulling her into the crowded carriage. 'All aboard!'

Thornton and Van Goole scrambled into the cab and the train engine roared into life.

Inside the train it was chaos, frightened children staring with wide eyes at the hissing, snarling creatures that advanced across the concourse towards the train. Everything started to vibrate and rattle as the engine began to move slowly away. Amy crossed her fingers. They were going to make it.

'Doctor!' One of the teachers suddenly pushed through the carriage, her face pale. 'Professor Willard and Mr Cain. They're not on-board.'

The Doctor stared at her in disbelief. 'What? Where are they?'

The teacher shook her head. 'He said something about getting his notes…'

'The idiot!'

The Doctor dived across to an intercom set in the carriage wall, and stabbed at the button. 'Van Goole!' he shouted. You've got to stop the train!'

'What?' came the startled reply. 'Have you gone mad, Doctor?'

'There's still two people out there! The Professor and Cain.'

There was a pause for a moment. 'I'm sorry Doctor, I can't risk the lives of everyone onboard for two people. They're on their own.'

Amy held her breath as she watched the anguish flicker across the Doctor's face. He had been so sure that he could get everyone away safely, so confident that no more people would die. A look of determination flashed into his eyes and in that moment Amy knew that he was going to get off the train to try and rescue the two teachers.

She opened her mouth ready to try and talk him out of it when there was a cry from one of the schoolchildren.

'Look! There they are!'

Amy turned and peered out through the train window. The professor and the tall supply teacher were racing across the concourse towards them. Willard was clutching a cylindrical container to his chest, his face crimson with the effort of running.

The Doctor raced to the back of the train, hurling open the rear doors. 'Come on!' he bellowed. Amy held her breath. The train was picking up speed, and whilst Cain's long legs meant that he was gaining with every stride, the little professor was struggling to keep up.

They were nearly at the train when there was

a sudden terrifying crash and the huge glass wall finally gave way under the weight of the creatures that had piled up against it. Glass and stones scattered across the floor as a tide of the creatures surged in through the jagged hole.

Startled by the noise, Willard stumbled, tumbling painfully to his knees on the platform. Cain gave the professor what looked like an apologetic shrug as he scrambled up on to the rapidly accelerating train.

Without a moment's hesitation the Doctor leapt down onto the platform, grabbing the professor by the arm and dragging him bodily to his feet. Behind them the creatures snarled and snapped, the sound of their legs clicking on the hard floor and the hissing whispering that they made echoing around the terminal building.

Amy's heart leapt into her mouth as one of them latched on to the professor's leg, making him cry out in pain and alarm. The Doctor tore it loose and threw it away, kicking out at the carpet of monsters that now spat and gnashed at their feet. He started to sprint down the platform half dragging, half carrying the professor. They were so close, but the train was picking up speed by the second.

Amy punched at the intercom. 'Slow down!' she yelled. 'Please! The Doctor has got the professor. You've got to give them a chance to get back onboard!'

A muffled curse came from the speaker. The train gave a sudden lurch, and children started to scream as bags and packages tumbled from overhead compartments. The train slowed and a dozen pairs of hands hauled the Doctor and Willard *on-board*.

'We've got them!' shouted Amy. 'Go, Van Goole! Go!'

There was a roar of engines and Amy had to hang onto a rail as the train surged forward once more. Behind them the terminal was now full to bursting with the creatures, hissing and screaming in frustration as their prey eluded them.

The train burst out from the terminal into daylight. Pebbles clattered down onto the carriage roof and for one horrible moment Amy thought that they had delayed their escape too long. Children and adults alike screamed as the claws of the creatures skittered onto the metal as they tried to get a grip, but as the train got faster and faster the creatures tumbled onto the desert floor. Within minutes they had left the rain of pebbles behind them.

Amy looked down to where the Doctor was slumped on the floor, breathless, glaring angrily at the gasping professor who was still clutching the container to his chest.

'You nearly got us killed, you know,' he snapped angrily.

'I'm sorry,' wheezed the professor. 'My notes.

My life's work. I couldn't leave them.' He glanced over at Cain. 'Too valuable.'

The Doctor said nothing, but the look on his face was plain for all to see. He scrambled to his feet, looking down at the frightened professor. Blood was seeping through the fabric of his trousers where the creature had caught hold of him

'You'd better get that looked at. Amy, can you get Rory to take care of Professor Willard? I need to see how Thornton is doing.'

Amy nodded. 'Okay.'

The Doctor turned and marched off down the carriage.

Amy bent down and helped the professor to his feet.

Mr Cain reached down and picked up the specimen box. 'I'll look after this for you, Professor. Would be a shame for it to go missing after all the trouble you went through to get it.'

Amy frowned as the two men exchanged

a glance. Somehow she had the feeling that there was more to the recovery of that box than they realised.

The Doctor pushed his way through to the front of the train, reassuring both children and adults alike that they had made it away safely. When he reached the engine he ducked down into the power compartment to check on Kevin and Matty.

'How are my engineers doing?'

Kevin looked up and gave him a nervous thumbs up. Matty was studying the dials intently, his hand hovering over the temperature control.

'It got a bit hairy when we were slowing down then speeding up again, but it's all under control now,' he said proudly.

'Never doubted you for a moment.' The Doctor grinned and ducked back out of the low door. Van Goole looked up as he entered the cab.

'What was that fool Willard playing at? He could

have got us all killed,' snapped the warden angrily.

'I told him the same thing myself.'

'Is he all right?'

'A bite on his leg, nothing too serious. Rory will sort him out.'

The Doctor sat down alongside the engineer, staring out through the plexiglass dome at the thin rail stretching out across the desert scrub. The train sped forward, with the faintest of clicks and clacks from the wheels. The sky was a brilliant blue, and long shadows cast from the trees turned the dry dust into a patchwork of subtle colours. It was difficult to believe that so much death and horror only lay a short distance behind them. But the Doctor knew only too well how quickly chaos and destruction could engulf even the most peaceful of places.

'How long will it take to reach the city?'

Thornton turned and gave him a half smile. 'Five, maybe six hours.'

'How long before we've got far enough away from the creatures for us to establish communications?' asked Van Goole.

The Doctor pulled out his sonic screwdriver and peered at the readings. 'An hour, assuming we can keep up this speed.'

'Ah, well there's the slight problem.' Thornton gave him an apologetic look. 'Some of the fuel cells are struggling with the load. There's a trackside shuttle pad about eight miles ahead. We should be able to pick up some back-up cells there.'

'We need to stop?' Van Goole frowned. 'Is that really necessary? Those things will gain on us pretty fast.'

Thornton shrugged. 'What would you prefer, stop for five minutes and have spare fuel cells, or keep going and potentially run out of power halfway to Ortagon City?'

Van Goole sighed. 'Put like that, I guess we have no choice.'

'Good.' The Doctor got to his feet, rubbing his hands. 'Plan A seems to be going splendidly. Now I want to make sure that we've got a plan B, just in case.'

'Plan B?' asked Van Goole curiously.

'Yes. A tribe of seventy families that seemed to know what was coming and seem to know where to hide. I'm going to have a little chat with our friend Attar.'

The Doctor ducked out of the cabin, almost colliding with a shadowed figure waiting outside the door.

'Doctor, I wanted to apologise,' said Cain sheepishly. 'What we did was appallingly dangerous, but the professor seemed so insistent about retrieving his notes. I simply couldn't let him go alone.'

The Doctor stared at him for a moment, then nodded. 'Apology accepted. Would you excuse me, Mr Cain? I'm in a bit of a hurry.'

Cain watched the Doctor make his way back towards the passenger compartments. Eager to find out what their situation was, he had followed the Doctor and waited outside the cab, listening as Thornton had explained about the fuel cells. A smile flickered across his lips. It was perfect. When they made their stop at the shuttle pad, he and Willard would make their escape.

Everything was working out perfectly.

Amy pushed open the door to the first class compartment that Rory and the others had turned into a makeshift medical bay and helped Willard onto one of the seats.

Rory hurried over, his face anxious as he caught sight of the blood.

'What happened? Are you all right?'

'Yeah, the Doctor decided to get off the train to help this muppet, but other than that...'

'Young lady,' spluttered Willard. 'Kindly show a little respect…'

'For you being so stupid?' Amy glared at him. 'Right, Professor. Really smart move.'

Any reply the professor might have made was cut off as he gave a yelp of pain. Rory had peeled back his tattered trousers and was examining a deep gash in his calf.

'That's going to need a stitch…'

'Do you want me to give you a hand, Doctor Pond?' said Amy mischievously.

'No, thank you. I need to concentrate. And shouldn't it be Doctor Williams?' said Rory indignantly.

'Whatever you say, doctor.' Amy looked around the compartment. 'How are you doing, anyway?

Rory gave her a tired smile. 'I'm coping. I've had a lot of scared kids to deal with. A few of the adults too. The boy with the broken arm is fine as long as he has a supply of chocolate. I'm just hoping that these bites don't get infected.'

'Infected!' squawked the professor.

Amy rolled her eyes. 'Great bedside manner, Doctor Williams.'

'Sorry! Didn't mean to say that out loud. I'll give you an antibiotic.' Rory fumbled in a medical kit and shot a look at Amy. 'I'm doing my best, you know.'

'I think that you're doing great.' She gave him a peck on the cheek. 'How about her?'

She nodded at where Gellen was curled up on one of the seats.

'Honestly, I don't know. She's still in shock. She needs rest and time to come to terms with what happened to her parents, not yet more stress. She just came in here and curled up as soon as we got away. She's exhausted.'

Amy gently brushed a strand of hair from the girl's forehead. 'Poor thing.' She knew something of what the girl might be going through. Suddenly being dropped into an impossible situation. Suddenly having to deal with monsters when you have had people telling you for your entire life that they didn't exist…

'Daydreaming, Pond?'

The Doctor was leaning in through the doorway, looking at her quizzically. She flushed.

'No. I was… thinking.'

'Good. Thinking's good. Been doing a lot of it myself. Hello Rory, glad to see you're taking good care of our professor. Careful with that wound. Nasty little teeth our friends have got. All sorts of bugs I wouldn't wonder. Probably best if you administer a broad spectrum antibiotic.'

Rory held up the hypodermic unit that he was preparing. 'Er, yes. Thank you. Not completely clueless.'

'Glad to hear it! He'll probably need a couple of stitches too. Now, Amy, any idea where your friend Attar might be?'

Amy shrugged. 'He was loitering at the back of the rear carriage, I think.'

'Well, we've no time for loitering. Come on. We need to get a peek inside his head!'

CHAPTER 7
MEMORIES OF THE PAST

Gellen was dreaming. It was a dream full of snapping teeth and whispering voices, of drowning in a sea of small, smooth shapes. She tried to pull herself free but the teeth started tearing at her clothes, her skin...

She jerked awake with a start, breathing hard. She looked around, reassuring herself that she was safe. But...

She frowned. Even though she was awake she was certain that she had heard the creepy whispering noise that the creatures made. She sat up, looking around the compartment. Rory was sitting over by the window, head slumped on his chest. He looked exhausted.

At the far end of the carriage she could see that there was someone standing next to the seat where the professor was sitting with his leg up. It was the teacher – Cain. He was speaking to the professor in a low, urgent voice. Gellen strained to try and hear what they were saying. Whatever it was, the professor didn't seem very happy about it.

Suddenly Cain leaned down, grabbed the professor by his jacket and hauled him to his feet. Gellen ducked back down onto her seat, pretending to be asleep as the two men hurried past her and out into the corridor. Cain was holding a bulky silver box, and as he passed her Gellen was certain that she could hear the whispering chatter of the creatures once more.

As the sound of footsteps receded she slipped

from her seat, craning her neck to see where the two men had gone. The limping professor was being bundled roughly through the doorway into the baggage car. She had to duck out of sight as Cain glanced back into the passageway.

For a moment Gellen wondered if she should try and wake Rory. But what would she tell him? It wasn't as though she had seen them do anything wrong. Even so, Gellen was certain that they were up to no good.

As she slumped back in her seat, wondering what to do, something sharp dug into her back. She reached around and pulled out the holo-recorder that her mother had given her. It had still been around her neck when she had been found. For one horrible moment her emotions threatened to overwhelm her. The death of her father and stepmother was still something that she could barely come to terms with. All that she wanted was to be back on Earth in her dad's little flat in Brighton.

She rubbed the tears from her eyes. If Cain and Professor Willard were up to no good, then this was her way of proving it. Slinging the holo-recorder around her neck she scurried down the passageway after them.

'Attar! There you are. Thought we'd lost you. Need to have a word.' The Doctor plonked himself down in the seat opposite the young native.

Attar was in no mood to play games.

'Leave me alone.'

'I need to find out where your people have gone and what their relationship is with these creatures.'

'And I've already told you that I don't know.'

'But I think you do.' The Doctor leaned forward, elbows resting on the table. 'You say that you were told stories when you were a child. An oral history passed down from one generation to the next. The story of your race.'

'But I've forgotten everything that I was taught!'

'No, it's just that you can't remember, there's a difference.' The Doctor reached out and tapped Attar on the forehead. 'Everything that we know is in there, we just need to get at it. Now…' He leaned back. 'These lessons, these stories. They start when you are very young, yes?'

Attar nodded. 'It is our first day away from our mothers. The old men would come before the sunrise, take us all to the Hut of Learning and sit us on the floor before the great paintings.'

'Good. Right, so it needs to be dark!' The Doctor jumped up and pointed his sonic screwdriver at the windows of the carriage. There was a whir of power and the glass darkened to a smoky grey. There were mutters of irritation from some of the adults in the carriage as they were plunged into darkness. The Doctor placed his sonic screwdriver in the centre of the table, his face dimly illuminated by the flickering green light at its tip.

'Right. What else. Are the stories spoken in verse, in prose, in tune?'

'There are drums…'

'A rhythm! Excellent!'

'But it's so long ago,' Attar said, shaking his head. 'I could never remember…'

'I know what the tune is…'

A nervous voice piped up from the darkness.

The Doctor turned to see a young girl peering at him over the seatback.

'Hello! Who are you then?'

'I'm Karen.'

'Karen who knows what the tune is.'

The girl blushed. 'I'm reading an i-book about it at school. I've got a copy with me.'

'Can we hear it?'

The girl nodded and ducked down behind her seat, emerging a few moments later with a compact computer pad. She tapped the screen and a low rhythmic drumming filled the air. 'It's only a modern recording. They never let people from outside the tribe into their ceremonies.'

The Doctor glanced over at Attar. The sound of the drums had obviously had an affect on the young man. Attar's eyes were slowly glazing. 'It's good enough for us,' murmured the Doctor, slowly drumming his fingers on the table in time with the recording. He gestured to the circle of children that was now clustered around them. Slowly the children started to pick up the rhythm, drumming on seat covers and chair backs, on books and satchels. The noise filled the carriage. Attar seemed to be dropping into an almost trance-like state.

The Doctor reached into his pocket and removed something small and disc-like.

'Attar, I want you to concentrate on this.' The Doctor leaned across the table once more. He had a small biscuit held between his thumb and forefinger. 'In an ideal world this should be a silver disk or a blue crystal, but a Jammie Dodger is the best I can do in the circumstances. I want you to watch it.'

The Doctor started to roll the biscuit between his fingers, like a magician with a coin, back and forth, faster and faster in time with the rhythm of the drums. Attar's eyes flickered back and forth as he followed the movement. The Doctor's voice was low and soothing. 'Concentrate on it, Attar. Concentrate and listen to the drums. Remember a time when you were young. Remember the Hut of Learning.'

Attar started to sway his head slowly.

'Do you remember the story that the old men told you?'

Attar nodded.

'Tell us, Attar,' whispered the Doctor. 'Tell us what you were taught.'

Attar took a deep breath. 'In the time before

time, the people of the plains lived in a mighty city…'

'What's that noise?'

Professor Willard looked up anxiously as the sound of drumming drifted through into the baggage car.

Cain shrugged. 'Probably nothing.'

'It sounds like Ulla ceremonial drums.'

'Will you concentrate!'

Cain had set the professor's specimen case on top of a plastic storage box in the baggage car. The professor was bent over the open case examining what was inside with an eyeglass. Cain stood well back from him.

'Are you sure they'll be dormant?'

'Yes, of course,' said the professor. 'There's a built-in stasis generator.' He lifted a piece of what looked like thin rubber from the box with a set of tweezers. It was bright silver. 'Extraordinary!'

'What is?'

'This material is like nothing I've ever encountered.'

'It doesn't look that special to me.'

'But it's metal. It conducts like metal, it has the strength of metal, but it's completely flexible.'

The professor looked at Cain in astonishment. 'Do you realise the applications of a metal like this?'

Cain took the tweezers from him and examined the silver material carefully. 'Yes. It means we are going to be very rich.'

'Not if we get caught by that swarm! And even if we do get to Ortagon City, how are we going to get this past the authorities without it being discovered?'

'Don't worry about that, professor,' Cain gave a cruel smile. 'I overheard the Doctor and the others talking in the cab. We're going to be making a stop at a shuttle pad in less than an hour. The

Doctor thinks that we'll be far enough away from the creatures to be free of that interference that they generate.'

'So?' the professor looked puzzled.

'So we're going to steal one of those shuttles and get far away from here.'

The professor gave a snort. 'Really, Julius, and who do you think is going to fly this shuttle?'

'You are. You're always going on about how you flew shuttlecraft during the Cyber War. Now's your chance to relive old times.'

The professor looked at him in disbelief. 'You're mad. We'll never get all these people on one shuttle.'

'Who's talking about everyone? I'm just thinking of you and me…'

'But we can't just… leave them!'

'That's exactly what we can do,' Cain spat angrily.

'And you think that they're just going to sit back and watch us leave?'

'You really don't have much faith in me, do you? When they were loading the train I noticed one of Van Goole's people putting a stun gun rack on board. Presumably they had the occasional problem with the local wildlife getting a bit too close to the terminal. It's got to be in this baggage car somewhere and you're going to help me find it. Then if anyone tries to stop us…' The look on Cain's face made it perfectly clear how far he was prepared to go, and how little patience he would have if the professor argued any further. With shaking hands, the professor put the lid back on the specimen box.

Gellen watched the two men through the night vision on her holo-recorder. She had snuck into the baggage car and hidden behind the large blue box that belonged to the Doctor, watching as Cain and the professor had argued, recording it all so that she could show Rory.

All she needed now was to get a shot of whatever it was that they had hidden in the specimen box. Although she already had a terrible suspicion of what she was going to find, she had to have proof.

Waiting until the two men had moved off into the darkness of a far corner, she snuck forward, keeping close to the wall, hiding in the shadows. She could hear Cain's gruff voice as he ordered the professor about at the far end of the carriage. This was her moment.

Sneaking forwards she darted across to the specimen case. With one hand keeping the holo-recorder trained on the lid, she reached out with her other hand and snapped open the clasps.

Heart pounding she lifted the lid and peered into the open box.

It was everything that she had feared.

Inside were three of the pebble creatures.

CHAPTER 8
TRAITOR ON-BOARD

The Doctor leant forward on the table, chin resting on one hand, nibbling on the Jammie Dodger and pondering everything that he had learnt from Attar. The native lad was slumped back in his seat, exhausted from his hypnotic ordeal. The kids had all drifted away, their momentary distraction gone. Amy sat quietly, waiting for the Doctor to say something.

Finally he looked up and gave a sad smile.

'Did you find out what you wanted?' asked Amy.

'Oh yes. I'm afraid I did.'

'Well?'

The Doctor shrugged. 'You heard what he said.'

Amy glared at him in frustration. 'It was very long and very garbled! Can you give me the short version?'

The Doctor gave a great sigh. 'Attar's people had a great civilisation here once. A technological empire...'

'Really?' Amy frowned. 'The huts we saw were made from straw and sticks. Hardly the height of technology.'

'Can I finish?' asked the Doctor.

Amy drew a finger across her lips.

'The planet developed to an advanced state very quickly,' continued the Doctor. 'Too quickly. They had power before they knew how to handle it. They rapidly exhausted their natural resources and brought the entire planet to the brink of ecological and economic disaster. Their last frantic attempt to stop total collapse was a biomechanical experiment.'

'The creatures?' Amy was aghast.

'Yes,' said the Doctor. 'They created a self-replicating machine-creature, a manufacturing machine, capable of processing any form of matter and recombining it into a multi-purpose mineral element. They thought that it was the answer to all their problems – but unfortunately they couldn't control it.'

'It destroyed them?' asked Amy quietly.

'In a way, yes. They realised that they had created a monster that they had no way of stopping, so they launched it into space. But the legacy of what they had created destroyed everything. They destroyed their cities, their factories, their entire way of life, so that such a monster could never be created again. With nothing left to trade, their entire way of life collapsed, the population reduced to a few scattered communities. Over the centuries they have all but forgotten who they once were, just a vague memory, kept alive by campfire rituals and children's stories.'

'Passed down from generation to generation.'

'A legacy, in case the creatures ever returned. And now they have.'

'But how?' asked Amy.

The Doctor shrugged. 'They launched the creatures into space in an unmanned spacecraft of some kind, probably aiming to send it into the Sun, or a black hole. Something went wrong. They missed. The spacecraft probably drifted for centuries before breaking up, either though collision, or an accident. They might even have been found and released by some unsuspecting space traveller.'

'And they've made it all the way back here?' Amy asked.

'A homing instinct of some kind. They've

probably destroyed hundreds of worlds on their journey home.' The Doctor's voice was sad.

'And they'll destroy hundreds more once they've finished here.'

'No.' The Doctor shook his head. 'No, it stops here.'

'How?' asked Amy, frowning.

'Because the people who built these creatures all those years ago also provided a way of destroying them. A machine. A fail-safe device in case they ever returned. A secret kept alive by Attar's people for centuries.'

'And you think that's where they've gone? To find this machine?'

'I'm certain of it.'

'Then what are we waiting for?'

The Doctor held her gaze. 'Because I'm going to need the train to get there, and to do that I've got to persuade Mr Van Goole that I'm right.'

Gellen was rooted to the spot, unable to tear her eyes from the pebble creatures in the bottom of the specimen box. Slowly it dawned on her that the creatures were asleep, or drugged. Whatever the reason, they showed no sign of movement.

Sudden anger welled up inside her. These were the things that had killed her father and stepmother. She felt a sudden urge to tip over the box. She wanted to smash them to pieces, crush them beneath her feet.

'Are these the things?' The sound of the professor's voice from the far end of the carriage made Gellen jump. She hurriedly slammed the lid back onto the box and scurried back to her hiding place.

The professor emerged from a pile of crates, holding a bulky handgun in each hand. Cain snatched one off him, snapping it open and peering down the barrel.

'Of course they are. What did you think they

were, kids' toys?'

'The case said that they were only stun pistols.'

'And so they are.' Cain snapped the gun shut with an unpleasant smile. 'But a charge big enough to bring down a Beslon is going to have quite an effect on something smaller.'

The professor stared warily at the gun in his hands. 'Are you sure that this is absolutely necessary?'

There was a sudden jolt and the train began to slow down.

'Grab your specimens, professor. Time to disembark!'

Gellen watched in horror as the professor hoisted the specimen case into his arms. As he did so, she realised that in her rush she hadn't done up all of the clasps properly. One of them was hanging loose!

The Doctor and Amy leaned out of the window,

watching as the train slid slowly to a halt at a narrow platform alongside the shuttle pad. The facility was even more basic than the terminal had been. The large circular landing pad was bordered with a cluster of small one-storey buildings and row upon row of cargo containers. A lone shuttle, its hull pitted and scarred from the constant cycle of lifting into orbit and re-entry gleamed in the afternoon sun. In the distance a range of snow-capped mountains loomed over the plains.

Puzzled technicians hurried forward to greet Thornton and Van Goole as they climbed down from the cab, and there was an animated conversation as the situation was explained to them.

'I'd better get out there,' muttered the Doctor. 'Thornton may well need help with those spare power cells.'

'I'll come with you,' said Amy, unwilling to let the Doctor out of her sight and eager for a chance to stretch her legs after an hour cooped up in the overcrowded train.

'Nobody is going anywhere,' came a voice from behind them.

The two of them turned to see Professor Willard and Mr Cain step through into the carriage from the baggage car, each of them holding a stubby gun.

Children screamed and tried to scramble away from them.

'Everybody sit still and keep quiet!' shouted Cain, waving his gun menacingly. He pushed his way towards the door, the professor following nervously behind him.

'What are you doing?' cried the Doctor. 'There's no time for this!'

'Not all of us are convinced by your escape plan, Doctor,' snarled Cain. 'Not when there's a perfectly good shuttlecraft to be had.'

'No, no, no!' The Doctor shook his head in

frustration. 'I've already explained to you. The creatures generate a gravitational interference field. Trying to take off would be appallingly dangerous.'

'Ah, but we've come a long way from that field, haven't we Doctor? I heard you talking to Van Goole. By now we're out of range of that interference field. Far enough for communications with Ortagon City to be re-established.'

'Don't be an idiot, Cain!'

'I've had enough of listening to you and your bright ideas, Doctor!' Cain raised the gun. 'Now get out of my way.'

Amy tugged at the Doctor's arm. 'Let them go, Doctor. If you're right, then they'll never get off the ground anyway.'

'But there's more to it than just escaping, isn't there?' said the Doctor sadly.

He glanced at the specimen case that the Professor had clasped against his side. 'It wasn't just notes that you went back for, was it professor? It was something else.'

Amy's eyes widened. 'He caught some of those creatures?'

'Yes,' said the Doctor grimly. 'And he thinks that it's going to make him rich. But it's not. I can't allow it.'

'You're not in a position to stop us. Now, I'm not going to ask again, Doctor.'

Amy held her breath as Cain's finger started to tighten on the trigger of the gun.

'Does anyone know why the train has stopped?'

Cain spun round in surprise as Rory hurried into the carriage. The Doctor seized the initiative and lunged for the gun but Cain was too fast for him. He lashed out, sending the Doctor sprawling in the aisle. The professor staggered backwards as the Doctor crashed down. As he did so he fumbled with the specimen case and it clattered to the floor, its lid sliding loose!

With a cry of panic the professor dived for it, slamming the lid back on.

With the two men distracted, Amy tried to make a break for it, but Cain caught hold of her roughly. She tried to break free but Cain was strong. An arm clamped hard around her neck.

'Sorry. Looks like you're going to be coming with us.'

'Cain, stop!' gasped the Doctor, staggering to his feet.

'What's going on?' Rory rushed forward, but Cain jammed the barrel of the gun against Amy's temple, warning him off.

'If you don't want anything unpleasant to happen to your girl, you just stay back.' He backed over to the door, sliding it open. 'Now, the professor and I are going to walk over to that shuttlecraft. No one tries to stop us and the girl stays safe.'

'No.' Rory shook his head. 'I'm not going to let

you take Amy.'

'It's all right, Rory.' Amy tried her best to sound confident. 'I'll be fine. Just do as he says.'

Cain grinned. 'Sensible girl. Come on, Willard.'

The professor hurried out onto the platform. Cain backed out after him, the gun still pointed at Amy's head.

The two men made their way towards the shuttle with Amy. The professor fumbled with a control panel and a small ramp swung down from the shuttle's nose. The Doctor and Rory could only watch helplessly as Amy was bundled inside.

'What are we going to do?' asked Rory.

The Doctor was grim. 'I don't know.'

Behind them, unseen under one of the seats, a smooth pebble lay motionless in the shadows.

Cain pushed Amy roughly into a seat in the cockpit.

'You'll sit there and won't move if you know

what's good for you.'

'You won't get away with this,' she taunted. 'You're never going to be able to get this thing off the ground.'

'She's right!' stammered the professor. 'This is madness! The interference...'

'They've managed to get communication back, haven't they?' snarled Cain. 'So get in that seat!'

The professor clambered awkwardly into the pilot's seat, peering bemusedly at the controls. 'It's all so much more complicated than it was in my day.'

Cain slipped into the scat next to him, still keeping a wary eye on Amy. 'They say it's like riding a bike, professor. Once you've learned you never forget. Now get this thing off the ground!'

The Doctor and Rory watched in despair as the shuttle's engines gave a belching cough, then roared into life.

Slowly the bulky craft lifted into the air, sending clouds of dust swirling across the pad.

'I thought you said that they wouldn't be able to take off!' cried Rory.

'Taking off isn't the problem,' the Doctor was earnestly studying the read-out on his sonic screwdriver. 'Staying in the air once they've got up there, however...'

The shuttle continued to gain height. In moments it was like a toy in the sky and Rory had to shade his eyes against the sun to keep it in view.

The distant roar from the engines suddenly changed in pitch, and the shuttle lurched alarmingly.

The Doctor grimaced. 'Sometimes I hate being right all the time.'

Cain grabbed the arms of his seat in alarm.

'What's happening?'

The professor was stabbing frantically at the

controls. 'We're losing computer control. It must be the interference from those creatures! The engines are misfiring!'

Beads of sweat were forming on his brow as he struggled to keep the little craft from bucking and swaying.

'Do something,' cried Cain.

'What do you think I'm trying to do?'

Warning lights started to flash all across the control console and then there was suddenly a moment of total silence as the engines cut out.

Amy hung on for dear life as the shuttle dropped like a stone.

CHAPTER 9
AMY IN DANGER

Rory watched in horror as the shuttlecraft started to arc through the sky, a thin vapour trail streaming behind it like the tail of a kite. For a moment it looked as though it would just crash straight into the mountainside, but at the last minute it turned, and slowly started to level out.

Rory held his breath as the little ship ploughed into the ground, sending up clouds of dirt and rock as it skidded to a stop.

Rory started to run. 'I've got to get over there!'

The Doctor caught hold of his arm. 'Rory! Wait!'

'She could be hurt.'

'And it must be two or three miles to the crash site. You're not going to be much help to her if you get there half dead from exhaustion.'

Van Goole and Thornton were running down the platform towards them. 'What just happened?' spluttered Van Goole. 'Who was in that shuttlecraft?'

'Professor Willard and Mr Cain.' The Doctor quickly explained what had happened. 'They've taken Amy as a hostage.'

'What the devil were they thinking?'

'Oh, I think it's our Mr Cain who's been doing all the thinking. He's realised that the creatures are unique and that the metal they produce has the potential to make him rich. What he hasn't realised is that he's not the first to think along those lines, and if he gets those creatures off this planet then all that they are going to bring is death and destruction.'

'Why are we standing here talking when Amy could be dying?' Rory exploded. 'We need to do something!'

'And whatever it is, we need to do it quickly,' Thornton nodded down the platform. On the horizon a dark cloud had appeared, getting closer with every second.

'Good God,' Van Goole paled.

'The bigger the swarm gets the more it eats, the more it eats the faster it moves.' The Doctor turned back to the warden. 'Van Goole. You said that when the monorail was first built you ran a branch line out to the caves.'

Van Goole nodded. 'The junction is just ahead. But we never finished it.'

'But it got as far as the mountains?'

'Yes,' the warden nodded.

'Excellent!' The Doctor clapped his hands.

'Then that's where we're heading! Get everyone onboard Mr Thornton!'

'Now wait just one minute, Doctor!' said Van Goole firmly. 'I'm very sorry about your friend, but that line is a dead end. We've no chance of getting to the mountains and back before that cloud reaches us. We have to keep going forwards to the city. It's our only chance.'

'You can't just abandon Amy!' shouted Rory.

'We're not going to.' The Doctor pulled him gently away from the warden. 'Mr Van Goole. That swarm is getting bigger and more ferocious by the second. If we run, if we get to the city and escape, then they will continue to spread until the entire planet is engulfed. Everything – every animal, every insect, every plant – will be consumed. The metal shell that they are creating will coat the planet, trapping the heat from the core. The temperature will rise, hotter and hotter, until the pressure gets too much and the planet explodes.

That explosion will send those creatures flying off into space again, to land on another world, perhaps a more heavily populated one, perhaps a planet whose people haven't yet discovered space flight and have no means of escape.'

The Doctor leaned close to the warden, keeping his voice low and calm.

'These creatures are a mistake, an accident. They should never have been unleashed on the universe. We have a chance to stop them here and now. I can do it. *We* can do it. But I need your help.'

'But the people on the train... the children,' there was uncertainly in Van Goole's voice.

'Attar's people, the Ulla, have hidden in the caves in the mountains. If I'm right then those caves hold the key to stopping those creatures.'

'If you're right...' Van Goole stood silently for a moment then nodded.

'All right, Doctor. So far you've been right

every step of the way, I see no reason to start doubting you now. Mr Thornton! Are those fuel cells loaded?'

Thornton gave him a thumbs up.

'Right,' said Van Goole. 'Let's get started.'

Amy woke with the harsh smell of scorched plastic in her nose. She opened her eyes and looked around the wrecked cockpit. She could barely believe that she was still in one piece.

Despite everything, she had to admit that she had been impressed with the way the professor had handled the situation. As soon as the engines had cut out, he had managed to gain control over the crippled shuttle for long enough to get it into a controlled glide. The landing had been hard, but it could have been an awful lot worse.

Amy unbuckled her harness and hauled herself out of her seat. Smoke was starting to drift through the cockpit. Every instinct told her to run while she had the chance, but she couldn't bear the idea of leaving either of her captors hurt and trapped in the wreckage. Cautiously she picked her way through the cabin. There was a groan of pain from in front of her.

'Professor?' Amy pushed aside a tangle of cables. The professor was slumped over the control panel. Amy squeezed in next to him, easing him back in his seat. He had a nasty cut on his forehead from where he had fallen against the windshield, but otherwise he seemed unhurt.

She looked around for something to stem the trickle of blood. The corner of a silk handkerchief stuck out from the breast pocket of the professor's jacket. She pulled it out and pressed it to his forehead. He winced in pain. Amy wished Rory were here. He always knew how to handle situations like this.

'Regular little Florence Nightingale, aren't you?'

Cain emerged from behind the co-pilot's seat, one arm hanging by his side, the stun pistol held firmly in his other hand.

Amy glared at him. 'Now do you believe that we're still not clear of the interference?'

Cain sneered unpleasantly. 'We all make mistakes. Yours was not escaping while you had the chance.'

'Not all of us are as selfish as you are, Cain.'

'And that's their mistake. You have to look out for yourself in this universe. No one else is going to.'

'And look where it's got you!' sneered Amy. 'You're worse off now than when you were on the train. At least there you had some chance of escaping.'

Cain shrugged. 'As I said, we all make mistakes. But I've still got the professor, the specimens and you as a hostage, so it's not a complete disaster.'

'And what are you going to do with us? The

professor's in no state to go very far and there are millions more 'specimens' just over the horizon!'

'Very true.' Cain peered out through the shattered windscreen. 'Fortunately, the professor has brought us down near the caves. We'll hide there until the swarm has passed and wait for the rescue teams to arrive.'

'Oh, give up!' pleaded Amy. 'It's over.'

'I'm getting tired of your voice!' snapped Cain, brandishing the stun gun menacingly. 'Now help the professor.' Amy bit her lip. The man's patience was obviously at an end and she had no idea what he might do if she pushed him any further.

Unsnapping the buckle, she helped the professor out of his seat and over to the airlock door. Cain operated the controls and the door creaked open. Amy took a breath as clean air rushed into the cabin, swirling the smoke around them.

'The entrance to the caves is about a hundred yards away,' said Cain, peering out through the hatchway. 'Don't forget those specimens, Willard.'

The professor leaned down for the box, swaying unsteadily on his feet.

'I'll get it,' said Amy.

'Oh, no,' Cain swung the gun to cover her. 'I'd rather the professor carried it, if you don't mind.'

'But he's barely able to walk!'

'Then you can help him. Now move!'

Cursing under her breath, Amy put an arm around the professor's waist, and helped him down the short ramp. The mountain loomed over them. Cain gestured towards a jagged opening in the rocks ahead of them. As they made their way towards it, Amy, staggering under the weight of the professor, glanced back over her shoulder.

In the sky behind them a dark cloud was appearing.

'Hurry up, Doctor,' murmured Amy. 'Whatever you're going to do, hurry up.'

'Come on Attar, wakey, wakey! Can't have you sitting there dozing all day! Things to do, places to go!'

Attar looked up groggily as the Doctor burst into the carriage.

He rubbed his eyes and stretched, his second joint making his arms bend in seemingly impossible directions.

'I had the strangest of dreams...' his eyes widened. 'I can remember...!'

'Yes, yes, yes,' the Doctor hauled him to his feet. 'You can relive your childhood later. All I need you to remember right now is where your people will have gone.'

'The caves,' said Attar firmly. 'There is a sacred cavern deep within the mountain, a place of safety if the swarm ever returned.'

'And from what you told me there is also a way to stop them. A machine of some kind.'

Attar frowned. 'I think so, yes. There is a text that has words that no one has ever really understood. A list of numbers…'

'A shut-down code for our toothy friends.' The Doctor grinned. 'Perfect. Come on Attar, we need to get to those caves.'

The Doctor turned to see Rory waiting in the doorway. 'Rory, I'm sorry I need you to…'

'Stay here,' said Rory, nodding slowly. 'I know.'

The Doctor gave a frown. 'No argument? No insisting that you have to come with me?'

Rory shrugged. 'There's no point, is there? You've already made up your mind that you're going to go after Amy without me. Arguing with you isn't going to change your mind. It's just going to waste time.'

The Doctor squeezed his shoulder reassuringly. 'I'll get her back safely, Rory, I promise you that.'

Rory tried to force a smile to his lips. 'I know.'

'Good man!' The Doctor spun back to face

Attar once more. 'Now, this cave, this secret place. I'm assuming that it's well hidden, otherwise it would have been swarming with eager school children, dull professors and interested tourists by now, am I right?'

Attar nodded. 'It's at the centre of the mountains, hidden within a network of tunnels and passageways.'

'A labyrinth. Excellent. You've got to love a good labyrinth. That's probably where the professor and Cain are heading too. The professor is bound to have some knowledge of the maze, even if he's not aware of the secret chamber. So, how do we find our way?'

'The path is shown in the great painting in the Hut of Learning...' Attar tailed off, his face falling.

'The painting that was taken when your people evacuated their village,' said the Doctor solemnly.

The two men stood silently for a moment,

staring at each other.

'What are you saying?' Rory's voice was desperate. 'Are you saying you won't be able to find where they've taken Amy?'

'There must be mile upon mile of passageways,' the Doctor paced up and down the carriage, thinking frantically. 'Electronic trackers are going to be disrupted by the swarm; even the sonic screwdriver is going to be affected as they get closer. I can probably rig up a pheromone scanner, powered by the electrical field of my brain, but that's going to take time, which we don't have. Perhaps if I use…'

'Rory's shirt!' exclaimed Attar, suddenly.

'What?' The Doctor stared at him, puzzled.

'The pattern on his shirt! It's copied directly from the Great Painting. I may have forgotten what the stories meant, but I still had an eye for a good design when I saw it.'

The Doctor hurried over to Rory, examining

the complex tangle of lines on the t-shirt with excitement. 'Looks like you're going to be more help that you thought, Mr Pond! Come on, shirt off!'

Rory struggled out of the shirt, covering his bare chest self-consciously as the children around him started to giggle. The Doctor snatched the shirt from him and started to trace a line through the tangle. 'Yes, this is perfect. Come on Attar, time we were off! Oh, and find yourself something else to wear, Rory. We don't want you catching your death, now do we?'

As the Doctor turned to leave, Rory suddenly called after him. 'Doctor! Amy bought one of these shirts too! The professor and Cain, they'll have their own map!'

The Doctor's smile faded. 'Let's just hope that they are too wrapped up in their own problems to realise what's right in front of them. Don't worry, Rory, we'll find them.'

As the Doctor and Attar hurried from the carriage, a pebble-like shape started to rock back and forth in the shadows beneath the seats.

With a sharp crack the pebble split open and thin, wiry legs started to emerge.

The stasis field in the lid of the professor's specimen box had been holding the creature in a state of suspended animation, but the effects were starting to wear off. Slowly the creature was coming back to life.

CHAPTER 10
THE MACHINE

Amy felt as though they had been walking in circles for hours. The tunnels were narrow and slippery underfoot, and constantly twisted and turned. Occasionally, they would open out into a wide cave, but almost immediately would narrow back down until she had to duck her head to avoid cracking it on the jagged rocks of the ceiling.

The professor was becoming an increasingly dead weight on her shoulder, groaning with pain every time she tried to hoist him upright.

Eventually the difficult terrain and stumbling professor got the better of her and, catching her foot on a rock on the floor, she crashed to the ground.

'Get up,' Cain stood behind her, eyeing her suspiciously, his finger hovering over the trigger of the bulky stun pistol. 'I told you, no tricks.'

'I tripped!' she glared at him. 'The professor is exhausted and so am I. How much longer are we going to go on traipsing around these tunnels?'

'That's up to the professor, he's the expert.'

Amy helped the professor onto a rock ledge where he sat breathing heavily.

'Well, Professor?' said Cain impatiently. 'You know these caves better than anyone. Where would your precious natives be hiding out?'

The professor rubbed his forehead, wincing as his fingers brushed over the cut.

'There are so many caverns that are sacred to

the Ulla. We've barely surveyed more than a dozen. It will take years of careful study…'

'Well we haven't got years! I want you to get me somewhere that has food, water and a fire. I've got no intention of spending the night trapped in one of these miserable tunnels.'

'And what if the natives aren't keen on sharing?' asked Amy.

'Let me worry about that. Now which way, Professor?'

Willard pulled a small, battered journal from his jacket pocket. 'Last year's expedition found some interesting Ulla artefacts in a cave a few hundred yards from here. That would seem like the logical place to start.'

'Right. Then let's move.'

The train pulled to a juddering halt and Gellen watched as the Doctor and Attar jumped down onto the dust-strewn platform and hurried towards the mountain that loomed over them. All of the other children, teachers and colonists were starting to make their way out of the train too, taking the opportunity to stretch tired limbs and get some much needed fresh air.

At the top end of the platform she could see Warden Van Goole and Mr Thornton talking urgently. Gellen had overheard enough to know that there was no more track for them to follow. If the Doctor couldn't find a way of stopping the creatures then they were all trapped.

Strangely, she wasn't frightened. There was something about the Doctor that made her trust him the way that she had never trusted anyone else. He had promised that he would make things better, and he seemed like a man who didn't make promises lightly.

Deciding that it was a good idea if she got some fresh air herself, Gellen started to make her way towards the door. As she did so, something rustled underneath one of the seats in front of her, and a strange whispering filled the air.

Gellen felt her blood chill. One of the creatures was on the train! Slowly she bent down so that she could peer under the seats. It took a few seconds for her to make out the shapes in the darkness, but there, tucked up against the wall of the carriage, was the unmistakable pebble shape of the monsters that had destroyed her family.

Heart pounding, Gellen started to back away. As she did so, the creature scuttled around to face her, gave an angry hiss and lunged forward.

Attar had to jog to keep up with the Doctor as he raced through the winding tunnels in the mountainside. The Doctor had Rory's shirt held out in front of him as if it were a treasure map. Occasionally, when they reached a branch or a T-junction, he would stop and peer at the design, nose practically pressed to the fabric, twisting the shirt this way and that (even turning it upside down) before giving a cry of triumph and darting off down another passageway.

They turned a corner to be confronted by a high rock wall. Attar gave a groan of disbelief. It was a dead end.

'So much for the design being a map,' he said miserably. 'Now what do we do?'

'No, no, no.' The Doctor was studying the design once more. 'You think that this is a rock wall, don't you?'

'Well it is!' said Attar.

The Doctor shook his head. 'You're meant to *think* that it's a rock wall, but it's a door.'

'You're mad.'

'Very possibly, but I'm still right about it being a door. What's this symbol?' The Doctor held out Rory's shirt, his finger pointing at a tiny geometric shape painted on the fabric.

'It's nothing,' said Attar. 'Just the name of one

of the ancient songs.'

'Can you sing it?'

'Now?' Attar looked puzzled.

'Yes, now.' The Doctor stood back and looked expectantly at him.

Feeling somewhat foolish, Attar started to sing, one hand beating on his thigh in a steady rhythm. He sang quietly at first, but as the words started to echo around the tunnel walls, and the rhythm started to build, he found himself caught up in the words of the ancient song that had been lost to him until the Doctor had revived the long forgotten memories.

When the song was finished, Attar realised that the emotion had brought tears to his eyes. He rubbed the wetness away with the back of his hand, shooting an embarrassed glance at where the Doctor was watching him thoughtfully.

'Was there any particular point to that?' asked Attar, unused to the strength of feeling that the song had provoked in him.

'Oh, yes,' said the Doctor, nodding towards the end of the tunnel. Attar turned and his jaw dropped in astonishment. The seemingly solid rock wall had vanished, revealing a set of steep stone steps that stretched down into the darkness. Glowing veins of rock lit the tunnel with an eerie greenish glow.

'It seems that the technology of your ancestors uses complex aural patterns as its basic operating system. Opening the door was just a question of finding the right aural key. The right tune.'

'So the songs we were taught...'

'Are the operating instructions for a machine that was built long ago as a fail-safe in case the creatures ever returned.' The Doctor gestured to the steps. 'Shall we go and find the rest of your people?'

Together the two of them vanished into the green-lit gloom.

'What's that?'

Cain looked up in puzzlement as the sound of a distant song echoed around the tunnels.

'It sounds like an Ulla tribal song,' said Professor Willard in astonishment.

'Like singing, do they?' asked Amy.

'Oh yes, I wrote a thesis on the songs of the Ulla.' The professor plumped up with pride.

'We can have the history lesson later,' hissed Cain. 'Right now I just want to know where that's coming from.'

Amy cocked her head on one side. It was almost impossible to tell where the music was coming from; the noise seemed to echo from everywhere around the tunnel walls.

Cain scrambled to his feet. 'It's coming from down here.' He gestured towards one of the tunnels. 'It looks as though we've found our elusive natives without needing your notebooks, professor.'

Almost as suddenly as it had started the music was gone, and the icy silence of the caves descended once more.

Cain jabbed Amy with the toe of his boot. 'Come on!'

'Hey!' Amy shouted. 'Cut that out!'

'Then move! I don't want to risk losing them.'

Amy helped the professor struggle to his feet, and they made their way towards the source of the sound.

Gellen screamed as the creature darted forward, its teeth snapping at her ankles. She reached up at a strap hanging down from one of the bulging luggage racks above her and pulled hard. An avalanche of cases, bags and boxes crashed down onto the creature, burying it.

With the trapped monster snarling and thrashing behind her, Gellen ran, pushing her way through the connecting door and into the carriage beyond. She burst into the makeshift hospital, startling Rory, who looked up at her in alarm.

'Gellen? What's the matter?'

'There's one of those things here…' explained Gellen breathlessly.

'What?' Rory jumped to his feet. 'On the train? How?'

'It must have fallen out of that case of the Professor's. I think it might be my fault.' Gellen felt tears starting to well up behind her eyes. Rory hurried forward and gave her a reassuring hug.

'Hey. It's the professor who was stupid enough to want to keep one as a pet, remember?' He peered out cautiously into the corridor. 'I don't suppose you've got any idea where it is now, do you?'

'I pushed a load of cases on top of it, but I don't think that will stop it for very long.'

As if on cue there was a clatter from the far end of the carriage and the creature scrambled out of one of the air conditioning ducts. Gellen huddled behind Rory as it sniffed experimentally at the air. It seemed much slower than the ones that had attacked the hotel, as if it was half asleep, or drugged in some way. Perhaps the professor had done something to it…

The creature started to make its way down the carriage towards them, claws making their familiar clicking sound on the metal floor. Rory backed away, looking around for anything that they could use as a weapon. Suddenly his eyes settled on something.

'I'm going to try and distract it,' he whispered. 'When I do, make a run for the front of the train. Try and find Van Goole, or Thornton.'

Rory snatched something up from the counter. It was the remains of a sandwich. Before Gellen could stop him, Rory tossed the sandwich onto the floor in front of the searching creature. It fell on it ravenously, teeth snapping, until nothing remained but crumbs. Almost immediately the creature started to shudder and vibrate, its legs snapping back inside its shell. Gellen knew that she should run but she couldn't take her eyes from what was happening in front of her.

With a sickening, wet, slurping noise a crack opened up down the centre of the creature's back and it fell into two jagged halves. Immediately the two halves started to bend and twist, and there was a hissing shriek that made the hair on the back of Gellen's neck stand on end. With the familiar cracking noise, the pebbles split open and the legs slowly started to emerge.

Rory shot Gellen an apologetic look. Now they had two monsters to deal with!

The Doctor and Attar stepped down into a vast cavern, filled with people and animals. In the centre of the cave a huge column of gleaming metal stretched up towards the roof, banks of consoles circling its base.

The Doctor clapped his hands together in glee. 'Now that looks like a monster neutralising machine if ever I saw one!'

They made their way towards the huge machine, the tribespeople parting silently ahead of them as they made their way forward. At the base of the machine a console had been adorned with fruit and flowers, the Great Painting propped up on a crude frame to one side. Three of the elders sat on the floor in front of the console. As the Doctor and Attar approached, they rose gracefully to their feet.

The Doctor held out a hand. 'I'm sorry to intrude, but I'm the Doctor. I wonder if I might talk to someone in charge…'

'I am Kren.' One of the elders took his hand and touched it to his forehead. 'And you have no need to apologise, Doctor. You have brought back to us one who we thought was lost.'

Kren smiled at Attar, who was hovering

nervously behind the Doctor.

'Welcome back, Attar. The very fact of your being here means that all that you had once forgotten has been returned to you. You are one with the people once more.'

Attar bowed his head. 'I was foolish. I thought that the old ways were unimportant. I know better now.'

'Yes, well, lovely as this reunion is, we do have a slightly more pressing problem. Lots of tiny little beasties, gnashing teeth, devastating the planet.' The Doctor peered up at the towering machine. 'The entire history of your people has led to this moment, so why haven't you fired this thing up yet?'

Kren stared at him solemnly. 'You are right, Doctor, the stories and songs that were passed down from my father and his father before him right back to the time before time were all for this moment. From the point that the first creatures started to fall upon our land once more, we knew that we must act according to the ancient texts. The Great Picture led us through the mountain, and the songs of the people revealed this place to us…'

He tailed off, shame and sorrow in his eyes.

'And?' asked the Doctor, nervously.

'And everything we were taught, everything we have kept alive through the centuries was for nothing. The people of this world are doomed. The machine no longer functions.'

CHAPTER 11

END OF THE LINE

As Gellen and Rory hurried through the engine towards the cab, a dark shape suddenly emerged from a small hatchway. For a moment Gellen thought that the creatures had somehow managed to get ahead of her, but then an irritated voice spoke.

'Are we going to be stopped here for long?' A boy about the same age as her was looking at her quizzically.

'You scared the life out of me!' she snapped.

'Sorry. It's just we've been down here for ages.

I think they've forgotten about us.'

'Us?'

The face of another boy appeared through the hatchway. 'This is Kevin.' said the first boy. 'I'm Matty.'

'Where are Warden Van Goole and Mr Thornton?' asked Rory.

The boy called Matty shrugged. 'I'm not sure. Outside somewhere I think. Why? What's going on?'

Gellen quickly explained about the creatures that were loose on the train. Kevin went pale.

'We'd better get out of here,' he started to scramble up out of the hatchway.

'No, hang on a minute,' Matty stopped him. 'You heard what the Doctor said. Those things could kill everyone.'

'Er, hello. They could kill us too!' Rory reminded him.

'Not if we're smart.'

'Oh, no,' Kevin frowned. 'Are you going to volunteer us for something dangerous again?'

'I've got an idea,' Matty smiled.

The Doctor sat thoughtfully on the stone steps at the base of the machine, listening as the last note of the Song of the People echoed around the vast cavern.

The machine remained silent and dark.

'You see?' Kren held out his hands in despair. 'We have tried time and time again, but without success.'

'So I see.' The Doctor leapt to his feet and started examining the ancient control panel. 'It's a lovely idea that your ancestors had. Build the machine in the mountain, put the hardware somewhere that it could survive the centuries without being disturbed, but put the software – the operating instructions – in the heads of the people, in the language, the songs, the culture.'

He turned to Kren, eyes alive. 'But languages evolve, particularly over the sort of time periods that we're talking about. People add their own verses to songs, add a new harmony here, an extra chorus there, a little 'pa-rup-pa-pom-pom' to liven things up. Unfortunately, the machine doesn't recognise those changes. It's running on an older operating system. But Attar here never learnt those songs, never memorised them. What I've revived in him is a race memory, a pure recollection of what those songs *should* be. Version 1.0 in fact!'

He grabbed Attar by the arm, sitting him down in front of the console and thrust a pencil and paper into his hands. 'Kren, I want you to sing the song again, and Attar, anything that seems strange, anything unfamiliar and out of place, I want you to write it down. Write the song as it should be!'

The Doctor turned to face the assembled tribespeople. 'Ladies and gentlemen. Once more with feeling, if you please.'

'Blow up the train?' Rory stared at Matty in disbelief. 'But you can't!'

'Why not?'

'Because it's probably very expensive!' Rory blustered. 'Besides, what if we need it to…'

'To what? We've reached the end of the line. There's nowhere left for us to go.' Matty's eyes were blazing with excitement. 'But if we can lure those things into the engine, Kevin and I can set the temperature controls so that the boiler will overload. We jump off the train and boom! No more monsters.'

'Lure them with what?' Rory asked dubiously.

'Sweets.' Matty held out a crumpled bag. 'Kevin's liquorish sweets.'

If Rory had any doubts about the plan, they

were banished by a loud hiss from the baggage car, and the clattering of dozens of clawed feet. The creatures were multiplying. If they were going to do anything they had to move quickly.

'Okay,' Rory nodded. 'I'll lure the creatures in. Do you know how to get the train moving?'

Matty nodded. 'I've been watching Mr Thornton. It's pretty simple.'

'Thank you very much,' said a gruff voice from behind them. Everyone turned to see Thornton clambering into the cab. He glared at them. 'No one is going to be driving this train except me, so you'd better tell me what this little council of war is all about!'

Gellen scurried forward. 'Those creatures on the train. It's my fault, I think, but Matty says we can trap them. Blow them up.'

Thornton stared at her thoughtfully.

'Does he now?'

'Er, it's quite urgent, actually,' said Rory.

'Monsters. On the train. Right now.'

Thornton turned round and pressed a button on the control panel behind him. There was a metallic clunk as all the doors locked.

Rory looked around in alarm. 'Not *quite* what I had in mind.'

'If these things are on the train then we've got to keep 'em here,' said Thornton. 'Matty's quite right. The boiler is our best weapon. It's a good plan.'

Matty swelled with pride.

'But Rory and I will deal with it. You kids, I've got another job for you.'

The tribe must have sung their song half a dozen times before Attar finally found all the parts that were not original. The Doctor snatched up the note and scanned it quickly. The changes were scarcely noticeable. A note here, an odd word there.

'Right Attar, it's up to you now.' The Doctor

smiled at him. 'You have to become the teacher. Teach them this new version of the song, and do it quickly.'

Attar nodded. 'We are fast learners, Doctor.'

Attar and the elders hurried off into the crowd. The Doctor looked nervously at his watch. If this didn't work then they were out of time.

Rory peered nervously into the baggage car. In the gloom he could hear the creepy whispering of the creatures as they communicated with each other. From the looks of things they had already found one of the crates of food that had been loaded into the car. That meant that there must be more than two of them by now.

Reaching into the bag, Rory threw a handful of sweets onto the floor. At once there was the clatter of claws and one of the creatures appeared from the shadows, hissing hungrily. It darted forward, devouring the sweets in a gulp. Two more of the creatures scuttled from the shadows, hissing and snapping. More and more emerged until there were about a dozen.

Rory started to edge backwards, throwing handfuls of sweets as he went, drawing the creatures after him. As he passed through the connecting corridor into the engine compartment, he could see Matty and Gellen peering in through the outside window. He just hoped that this was going to work.

Gellen watched as Rory lured the creatures out of the baggage car and into the front of the train. As soon as she was certain that all of the creatures had followed him, she pulled open the door and Matty helped her scramble up into the baggage car.

The carriages were all separated by a set of sliding doors. Gellen pressed the red 'close' button and the glass partition hissed shut. She took the key that Mr Thornton had given her and slid it into a socket next to the button. There was a heavy clunk and a red light lit up over the door.

Gellen jumped back down from the train and gave Matty and Kevin a thumbs up. Matty grinned back at her and ducked under the carriage. There was a series of buttons, just as Thornton had told him. Kevin fumbled with a torch and a dull yellow glow illuminated the gloom. Matty peered at the crumpled bit of paper that Thornton had written his instructions on.

'Here goes.' With a silent prayer he pressed the buttons in the sequence indicated and there was a satisfying hiss of hydraulics as the engine uncoupled from the carriages.

Slowly the engine started to move away from the rest of the train. Matty and Kevin scrambled back up onto the platform alongside Gellen as the engine started to move off.

'Hey, you kids!'

Warden Van Goole hurried over as the engine started to pick up speed.

'What the devil is going on? Who's driving that thing?'

'Rory and Mr Thornton,' said Matty, checking his watch. 'But they'd better get off within the next two minutes.'

The song of the people started slowly, a low rumble of voices keeping steady time with the drums. Gradually it started building, more and more voices adding to the harmony until the cavern echoed with music. It was a song that had been sung countless times over the centuries, but today, it was different, today it was being sung as it had originally been written, pure and strong, a remnant of a distant time.

The Doctor stood in front of the control console of the huge machine, watching in admiration as mechanisms that had lain dormant for centuries slowly started to spring into life. Lights glowed on the control, read-outs flickered and a deep, throbbing hum started to build deep within the mountain, rising in tone as the music swelled.

'It's working,' breathed Attar.

'Yes,' the Doctor flexed his fingers like a concert pianist about to give a recital. 'Millions of years and all systems go.'

'This will stop them?'

'Oh, I think so. This machine sends out a powerful counterwave at the opposite end of the gravitational scale to the creatures' interference generators. That will disrupt their internal bio-electric power systems and put their cores into meltdown.'

Attar looked at him blankly.

'It'll scramble their innards.'

The Doctor peered at the read-outs. 'Ha-hah!' He rubbed his hands in anticipation. 'We seem to be at optimum power. Let's bring this nasty little plague of locusts to an end.'

The Doctor was reaching out for the control when a gunshot echoed around the cavern.

He spun around to see Cain, the professor and Amy on the steps at the far side of the cavern. Cain levelled the gun at Amy's head.

'Make any attempt to touch that switch, Doctor, and the girl is dead.'

CHAPTER 12
FINAL SOLUTIONS

Rory stared out of the window as the train picked up speed. Behind him, in the engine compartment, the creatures snapped and hissed as they divided, gorged on the sweets that had lured them in.

'Right,' said Thornton. 'We'd better get off before we run out of track.' Rory nodded. The end of the line was frighteningly close.

The engineer stabbed at a button and the cab door unlocked with a clunk. Rory stared at the ground whizzing past below them. This had seemed like a good idea when they were stationary.

'Bend your knees when you land,' said Thornton encouragingly. 'And roll with the fall. You'll be fine.'

'Done this a lot have you?' asked Rory.

Thornton just grinned. 'You'd be surprised.'

Rory was steeling himself to jump when something small and black came racing across the cabin floor. Thornton gave a bellow of pain as the creature clamped onto his leg. Rory looked in horror as more of the creatures gathered in the doorway. The boiler was now hissing and screaming. They could only have a matter of seconds!

Rory looked around frantically. There was a fire axe in a glass case by the doorway. Rory smashed the glass with his elbow and snatched the axe from its case.

'Thornton, keep still!'

Rory swung the axe like a golf club, catching the creature square on and sending it clattering off the cabin ceiling. Thornton gave a bellow of pain as the creature was torn free from his leg.

Throwing the axe to one side, Rory grabbed the engineer by the collar and hauled him out through the doorway.

They hit the ground hard, rolling over in the dust, winded by the impact. From behind them a loud hissing noise started to build, louder and louder until, with a deafening explosion, the train exploded.

Rory clasped his hands over his ears as the shockwave sent debris flying. His ears ringing, Rory looked around to see gouts of flame and thick black smoke billowing into the sky. The engine was on its side in the dry dirt, split open down the middle. Rory scrambled to his feet, watching anxiously for any sign of movement in the wreckage. To his relief there was nothing. They had done it. The creatures were dead.

relief there was nothing. They had done it. The creatures were dead.

There was the sound of cheering from behind him. Rory turned to see Gellen, Kevin and Matty leaping up and down on the distant platform, whooping and hollering in triumph. Rory smiled and waved. Then froze.

All the time that they had been preoccupied with the creatures that had got on-board the train, they had forgotten the ones that were pursuing them. Now the swarm cloud dominated the horizon. They had managed to kill a dozen of the creatures, but they had no defence against the millions that had now caught up with them.

'Hello, Pond,' the Doctor gave Amy a brief wave. 'How are you doing?'

'Oh, you know,' Amy shrugged. 'Kidnapped, been in a shuttle crash, got a gun pointed at my head. Other than that… You've been having a nice sing-song in the meantime, have you?'

The Doctor gave a wry smile. 'Something like that.' He watched as Cain led her slowly through the crowd of natives. 'Mr Cain. I need you to listen to me. I can stop this here and now. This machine will shut the creatures down, totally. Destroy them once and for all.'

'Then that sounds like a very good reason not to use it,' Cain waved the gun at him. 'Move away from the controls, Doctor.'

Professor Willard was staring up at the towering machine in awe. 'I don't believe it. This is stupendous. An archaeological goldmine.'

'Professor,' the Doctor kept his voice low and calm. 'Tell him. Make him understand. We have to stop these things.'

'It's no good, Doctor,' Cain shook his head. 'The professor isn't going to help wipe out an entire species, not when that species has the ability to make us both so much money.'

'But they're not a species,' said the Doctor sharply, his eyes fixed on the professor. 'They're a machine.'

'A machine?' A frown flickered over the professor's face.

'Yes, a manufacturing machine built by people who were blinded by greed. People like Cain. They can't be reprogrammed, they can't be controlled, they can only destroy, and they will keep on destroying unless we can turn them off. The Ulla unleashed them on the universe, but they also had the foresight to provide the way of stopping them. Are you really going to let an entire planet be destroyed, Professor? An entire solar system? An entire galaxy? How much money will it take for you to be able to forget the millions that will be killed by your actions here today?'

Willard turned, looking at Cain with uncertainty in his eyes. 'Julius?'

Cain pushed the professor out of the way angrily, swinging the gun to cover the Doctor.

'Very clever, Doctor, appealing to the professor's better nature. It might work with him, but it's not going to work with me. Now, I said, step away from the controls.'

'Julius, no, he might be right…'

'Shut up, Willard! I've stood by and watched enough people get rich around me. This time it's my turn.'

'I'm sorry Mr Cain,' said the Doctor firmly. 'But I can't allow these things to spread any further.'

'Then I'm going to have to kill you, Doctor,' said Cain.

'I know,' the Doctor nodded, his hand reaching towards the button on the console.

'No! Julius, no!'

The professor lunged forward, knocking Cain's arm as his finger tightened on the trigger. The stun gun went off with a deafening crack, sending a burst of energy zinging towards the cavern roof. Amy ducked as the two men struggled on the steps, energy bolts sizzling around them as the professor tried to wrestle the gun from Cain's grasp. With a savage blow, Cain knocked the little professor to the floor.

Winded, he stared up at his one-time friend. 'I'm sorry Julius, but I'm not going to let you do this.' He fumbled with the controls on the side of the specimen box. There was a beep as the small read-out screen changed from 'stasis' to 'revive'. Cain's eyes widened with horror as the professor undid the clasps on the lid.

The creatures practically exploded out of the box.

Cain and the professor didn't stand a chance. The ravenous creatures attacked with a terrible ferocity. The tribespeople scattered in panic as the gorged monsters started to shake and split, multiplying with frightening speed.

'Doctor!' screamed Amy. 'Now would be a good time!'

The Doctor took a deep breath and started to sing. As the machine recognised the tune, the button on the console lit up a fiery red.

The Doctor slammed his hand down.

Rory watched helplessly as the swarm of creatures surged forward. To have come so far, to have got this close to safety...

His only thought was of Amy. He just hoped that inside the mountain she was safe.

He closed his eyes.

There was a sudden deafening noise, like a

chord played on a vast church organ. Rory gave a cry of fear that was totally drowned out by the booming sound. Almost as suddenly, there was silence. Cautiously, Rory opened his eyes. Ahead of him, for as far as the eye could see, the ground was littered with the creatures, motionless, silent, just like rocks.

'What happened?' asked Thornton numbly.

'I think the Doctor happened,' said Rory.

The rescue shuttlecraft had already started to land by the time the Doctor, Amy and the Ulla finally emerged from the mountain.

As the tribe started to sing a song of celebration at their escape, Rory hurried over to Amy and gave her a huge hug. 'I thought I'd lost you. Again.'

Amy gave him a kiss on the cheek. 'Not a chance.'

'Oh, no! What happened?' the Doctor was

staring in dismay at the burned-out remains of the monorail engine. He turned to where Matty and Kevin were standing. 'I put you two in charge to make sure that that sort of thing didn't happen!'

'Sorry. But we didn't have a lot of choice,' said Matty, looking sheepish. 'It did make a fantastic bang though.' He broke into a huge grin.

'You remind me of a friend I once had,' said the Doctor frowning at him. 'She was always one for a big explosion too,' he sighed. 'Ah well, I guess everyone is going to have to get the shuttle back to Ortagon City instead.'

He looked around, searching for Gellen amongst the crowds. To his relief he could see a nurse helping her towards one of the shuttles. Crisis over, she had finally allowed herself to give in to the grief and sorrow. The Doctor gave a sad smile. It would be hard for her, but with time, the bad memories would fade. She was lucky, she still had family at home who would care for her, help her to heal.

'Looks like I was right to trust you after all, Doctor,' said Van Goole, walking over and shaking him warmly by the hand. 'Where's the professor? And our friend Mr Cain?'

The Doctor shook his head sadly. 'The professor finally decided that he was on our side after all, but too late I'm afraid.'

Van Goole sighed. 'I'm sorry.'

'I am too.'

The Doctor wandered over to where Attar was standing at the edge of the huge pebble desert that now stretched out towards the horizon. In the distance, a thin line of gleaming metal glinted in the setting sun.

'What do we do now, Doctor?' Attar asked. 'What do my people do?'

'You rebuild,' said the Doctor quietly. 'The metal that is out there is unique now that the machine that created it has been destroyed. The money it will bring should be enough for the Ulla and the colonists to rebuild this world.'

He turned to the young native.

'But you need to remember this day, Attar. The monster that was created here must never be allowed to live again.'

Attar nodded. 'I know, Doctor. We must not forget our past, we must learn from it.'

The Doctor nodded.

'You'll make a fine storyteller, Attar.'

Attar grinned. 'Well I wasn't exactly making a fortune selling t-shirts, was I? Let's see if I'm any better at writing songs.'

The Doctor patted him on the shoulder and turned to where his two companions were waiting for him.

'Come on, you two. Let's go and retrieve the TARDIS. I promised you a party, and I think we've earned one, don't you?'

Amy nodded. 'Couldn't agree more. Just one condition though…'

The Doctor looked at her quizzically.

'We go somewhere where they aren't playing rock.'

THE END

DOCTOR ☒ WHO

The journey through time and space never ends...
For more exciting adventures, look out for

Coming soon...
MONSTROUS MISSIONS and **STEP BACK IN TIME**

WANT MORE ACTION? MORE ADVENTURE? MORE ADRENALIN?

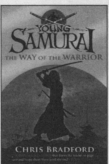

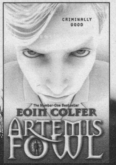

GET INTO PUFFIN'S ADVENTURE BOOKS FOR BOYS

Young Bond, *SilverFin* and Eye Logo are registered trademarks of Danjaq, LLC, used under licence by Ian Fleming Publications Limited

GET INSIDE YOUR FAVOURITE BOOK

spinebreakers.co.uk

spine breakers

spinebreaker (n)

story-surfer, word-lover, day-dreamer,
reader/ writer/ artist/ thinker